THE
Mirage
TREE

KARIN ELIZABETH R SMALE

Published by
Karin Elizabeth R. Smale
© 2018 Karin Elizabeth R. Smale
karin.smale@yahoo.com

The Mirage Tree: ISBN 978-0-6484000-7-3
The Mirage Tree eBook ISBN 978-0-6484000-6-6

Acknowledgements

To my family, Karen Mc Dermott and her amazing team and
the loyal friends who have been there for me over the years,
no matter what and despite everything,
just *damn well won't give up* ~

THANK YOU.
I love you.

To Sisters Everywhere.

*'I want everybody in the world to be on one page.
A page titled love.'*

Michael J. Jackson

1

Lost

Bitingly cold January air numbed her face. The air had a still, silent quality, the sky an expanse of steel grey flecked with white and the promise of yet more snow. A lingering sombre aura cast a wide shadow of post-Christmas disenchantment, at once both bleakly depressing and glamorously dazzling as a thick, smooth blanket of white transformed the Dartmoor landscape she had known all her life into an unfamiliar, shimmering fantasy world.

The blanket muffled all of nature, creating an almost unnatural serenity, which spread through the entire world. In sharp contrast, an escalating turmoil of anxiety welled up inside her, like a snowball rolling ever faster, out of control and increasing with every passing second. A rush of dizziness threatened to overwhelm her as she started to panic; she desperately surveyed the monotonous white canvas that stretched endlessly around her.

Gretchen! Where was she?

A dreadful sense of foreboding flooded Lauren's senses.

Clumsily, she began to run through the thick gorse, panic forcing renewed strength in her limbs, pushing her forward despite the heavy outdoor clothing.

Silence filled the brittle air. The only sounds were the breeze whipping around her head, the crunch of fresh snow under foot and the sharp rasping of her own breath.

How could she have been so stupid? Why hadn't she waited for the milder weather to take her precious puppy on her first outing? The snow had made everything so inviting and serene, enticing her to venture outside with the false promise of tranquillity and joy.

'Gretchen!' she called, but there was no answering yip and Lauren caught back a sob.

The little bundle of fur had won her heart from the first moment she'd seen her. The thought of losing her was unbearable. *This couldn't be!* Whatever would she do without her? Lauren's mind fleetingly wandered to the long evenings filled with solitude she had known since moving back home to Devon before adopting Gretchen. She'd recently come to terms with being single and Gretchen's company had made the transition much easier. Immediately she felt a cold band squeeze her heart; she certainly didn't want to go back to such loneliness again.

She hadn't intended to go far, just to the edge of the local moorland. It had been delightful to watch her little German Shepherd girl explore the snow, her sturdy little legs carrying her joyfully, trying to catch the flakes that mysteriously disappeared and shaking the cold white powder from her paws with a quizzical expression. She had looked so appealingly cute, so puzzled as if trying to work out where the strange white crystals went. Lauren couldn't resist snapping photo after photo until the phone call interrupted her.

She bit down on her lip hard, forcing herself to concentrate. If only she hadn't allowed herself to be distracted. It had only taken a few moments to answer her assistant's query about an order from her florist shop. Surely Gretchen couldn't have gone far? But what if it had been long enough for her to become lost? Confused and overwhelmed by the dazzling landscape? Lauren's heart pounded in her chest as she thought of the River Walkham, deep and now dangerously swollen with a menacing undercurrent after the long winter months. What if Gretchen had wandered to the edge and tumbled into the water?

Desperation gripped her now. Tasting saltiness, Lauren realised she had torn away a piece of skin from the inside of her lip. She forced her leaden feet to carry her through the fresh, powdery snow which moments before had seemed so enticingly picturesque, but now had become a loathsome hindrance.

'Gretchen! Where are you? *Gretchen!*'

Lauren approached a clearing. Stopping to catch her breath she noticed the rush of wind that had been ringing in her ears had ceased. Silence enveloped her, momentarily pierced by the shrill cry of a hunting Kestrel, swirling gracefully on a thermal high above her. The freezing air stung her throat and chest as she inhaled deeply, her escaping breath visible as a fine mist steadily rising in front of her, like steam from a hot drink. Lauren had thought herself reasonably fit, but forcing her heavy limbs onward through the thick snow had left her breathless.

'Hi there!' A friendly young male voice cut through her anxious speculation.

Lauren's legs felt weak as an immediate wave of relief struck her. A tall, athletic lad of around seventeen years old with dark hair, tanned skin and a perfect white smile strode towards her with ease, making furrows in the blanket of thick fresh snow. In one hand he held a leather lead and in the other was carelessly tossing a worn red rubber ball. A black and white Springer spaniel jumped gleefully in front of him in excited anticipation of a game.

Close behind the lad, up to her chest in snow stood little Gretchen, looking as if butter wouldn't melt in her mouth.

'There you are!' Lauren scooped up her little wanderer and cuddled her close.

'She's a bright little thing, isn't she?' the youth grinned. 'I love shepherds. I'm Josh Harrington…nice to meet you!' He cheerfully extended his right hand towards her in welcome. 'Charlie here never misses an opportunity to make a new friend. He went wandering and came back with her.'

Lauren allowed the squirming bundle of fur to return to the ground and accepted his handshake. 'Lauren Sinclair. I'm very glad she's safe,' she replied, her manner careful and reserved.

'Of course she is! We've been having a really good game and Charlie here has taken a real shine to her.'

He raised his arm and effortlessly shot the ball into the distance. Charlie bounded after it and little Gretchen took off after him, doing her best to keep up. Gleefully yipping in unison, they both disappeared into the snowy landscape.

Lauren was about to take chase when Josh's laughter stopped her.

'You're a bit out of breath there!' he teased. 'You couldn't catch them if you tried!'

Lauren glared at him. The nerve of the lad! It was bad enough he'd enticed her puppy away without him being impertinent as well.

As soon as the dogs returned from their game, she bent

down and called Gretchen, who obediently ran to her.

'She's too young to run so far from me,' she said, her voice shaking slightly as she slipped her fingers through the soft fur beneath the pup's collar. 'We must be going.'

'Aw, don't be such a spoilsport – just one more throw!'

'OK, but not quite so far this time please.'

The ball shot through the air like an arrow from a bow and the two dogs took off in elation, running far out of sight.

Suddenly a sharp yelp pierced the freezing air, followed by a mournful cry.

Gretchen!

Was she injured? Shooting the lad an angry look, Lauren bolted after the cry. She found Gretchen behind a snowdrift, lying motionless on her side.

Charlie dropped the ball and nosed at his little companion anxiously. Lauren bent over her puppy and ran her hand over her fur. Seconds later, Josh appeared effortlessly at her side.

'Is she OK?' He looked so upset Lauren's anger instantly dissolved.

'I don't know…she can't put any weight on her front leg. I must get her to a vet.'

'Come with me…I can help. I live just over there.' He gestured to a small grey cottage in the distance. A stream of smoke snaked thinly from the chimney.

'Well…if you're sure…' Her voice trailed as she suddenly became very aware of their isolation. The village and nearest vet were over five miles away.

'No problem! I have a first aid kit and I can get you to a vet. Here, give her to me, I'll carry her for you.'

At four months old, Gretchen already weighed nearly sixteen kilos. It would be a struggle for Lauren to carry her, and there wasn't another building for miles. Besides, it was his fault Gretchen was injured. Helping was the least he could do.

'Thank you,' she said.

Josh wrapped Gretchen in his jacket and effortlessly scooped her into his arms, setting a steady pace over the moors towards his home.

Lauren followed, concern for Gretchen driving her urgently over the few hundred metres to the cottage. Feet crunching into the snow and sinking several inches with each step, she willed her tired legs to carry her through the snow as quickly as possible.

As they approached the wooden gate of the modest granite and slate-roofed cottage, Josh slipped a small silver phone from his jacket pocket. He used speed dial and Lauren caught a few muttered words of the one-sided conversation.

'An accident…yes….you can come? OK…see you then.'

He unlocked the solid oak door with one hand while the other supported Gretchen's weight and kicked it open effortlessly. They entered a small cosy lounge. Warmth and a smoky pine aroma wafted over Lauren. A faded red rug covered worn oak floorboards and a sagging but comfortable looking couch, worn and threadbare in patches, sat next to a glowing fire behind a soot-blackened guard. Coloured scatter cushions in bright hues gave the place a cheery feel and a heavy oak table and dining chairs occupied the far side of the room.

On the wall, at a slightly jaunty angle, was a framed photograph of Josh and two other people. A strikingly handsome man in his early forties rested a hand on Josh's shoulder and an attractive, slim woman stood slightly apart from them. She had the longest, glossiest dark hair Lauren had ever seen. They must be his parents, she supposed. *Lovely family*. All three smiled cheerfully out at her in the dim light of the cottage. Through an archway that opened into the kitchen she spied a large tabby cat curled up on a chair in front of an old Rayburn. This modest little cottage may be shabby, but it certainly had a homely feel.

Josh ducked his head through the low door frame and gently laid Gretchen on the old couch, mindful of her injured leg. Kneeling beside her, he carefully moved the injured limb.

'Hmm…no…I don't think it's broken…' he muttered. Then, turning to Lauren, he offered, 'Here, let me take your jacket.'

'Shouldn't we be going to the vet?' What were they waiting for? Her puppy needed help *now!*

Josh sat back on his heels. 'Relax, it's not a problem. He'll be here shortly. Make yourself comfortable and I'll put the kettle on.'

'You've arranged for the vet to come here?' she asked, surprise adding a lilt to her voice. 'All the way out here, in this weather?'

'Yep. Like I said, it's no problem. My Dad is on another call, he's had a busy day, but he'll be here soon.'

'Wait – your father is a vet? Why didn't you tell me?' Lauren exclaimed.

'I'm telling you now. Besides, you didn't ask.' He grinned at her astonishment, clearly pleased with himself.

'Oh. I see.'

'I'll make that tea.'

Lauren shook her head. 'Don't worry about it. I'm fine. Let's just wait for your dad.'

She settled on the battered couch next to Gretchen, softly reassuring her and smoothing her fur. They sat quietly. The only sounds breaking the silence were an occasional crackle from the fireplace and the ticking of the clock on the mantelpiece counting down the minutes.

Before long there was a droning noise in the distance and the sound of a vehicle labouring slowly along the drive way gradually became louder. The engine stopped and as the car door slammed both Josh and Charlie jumped up and rushed to the door. Lauren glanced at the window. A tall figure clad entirely in grey and carrying a black leather medical bag was walking along the path towards the cottage, his head bowed against the weather.

She could hear a few muffled greetings at the doorway and the burden of worry lifted. 'It's going to be OK' she murmured, ruffling the soft fur behind Gretchen's ears. 'You'll feel better soon, the vet is here now.'

Thank goodness he'd arrived safely. She'd had her doubts with the weather being so bad.

'Lauren Sinclair?' His voice, deep and smooth as caffè latte, interrupted her thoughts. 'I'm Greg Harrington. It's a pleasure to meet you.'

She was instantly captivated by the figure that completely filled the entrance. It was rude to stare but she simply could not tear her gaze away from him. Looking directly back at her was the handsome man from the photograph; the same gorgeous white smile, the same smoothly tanned skin. His classic good looks were even more striking in real life. She had just seconds to take in his strong jaw line and rain-slicked dark hair, glossy and finely streaked with silver at the temples, before he strode confidently towards her with his hand extended in greeting. At just over six feet tall, he had a huge presence in the small room, yet a surprisingly lithe and gentle demeanour, which fascinated her.

'It's nice to meet you too. Thank you very much for coming

out here in this weather.' Lauren managed to keep her voice steady as she held his gaze. Despite his sincere expression, his eyes, deep and dark as mahogany under thick lashes, twinkled with a slight roguishness that momentarily took her breath away. His smile when it came was wide and friendly and Lauren was reminded of Josh's smile as he was throwing the ball for Charlie. The similarity was striking.

The vet took her hand and held it for a moment longer than was necessary before turning his attention to Gretchen. 'Ah, yes. Here's our little patient.'

He dropped to the puppy's side with ease and stroked the fur on her back, gently massaging away any anxiety and examined her joints. Producing a stethoscope from his bag, he smiled as Gretchen's natural curiosity got the better of her and she sniffed at the peculiar object, then licked his hand briefly and rolled over graciously to let him place it on her chest. Lauren marvelled at the skilful way he tended to her, with unhurried patience and compassion.

Slowly and with great care he moved to Gretchen's injured leg, concentration etched onto his face. After a few thoughtful moments he reached into his bag and deftly withdrew the contents of a tiny glass bottle into the syringe with a practiced manner.

He had elegant hands, Lauren observed. Precise and gentle, like a pianist.

All his movements were smooth and polished. Mesmerised, she watched him work. His skill was reassuring.

'It's not broken,' he said after a few moments. 'Just badly sprained. I'll give her a steroid and analgesic injection for the pain and swelling and leave you some anti-inflammatory tablets to be taken twice a day, morning and evening. They should do the trick.'

'Well, that's a blessing.' Relieved, Lauren stooped to stroke Gretchen's head. She smiled at the vet. 'I am so grateful for your help, Mr Harrington. Thank you so much.'

He returned her smile and Lauren's heart skipped a beat.

'Call me Greg, please. Well, we had better get you home, there's likely to be a storm this evening.' He indicated the view through the window and the now menacing steel-grey sky. Rolling opaque clouds, threateningly low, were already darkening the crisp, clear afternoon light to an icy - grey gloom.

'Come on, I'll drive you home before it gets worse out there. I'll just pack up my bag. Josh, please would you carry Gretchen to my car?'

'Let's have the patient.' Josh carefully lifted Gretchen, who turned her molten chocolate brown eyes to him with a look of self-pity and licked his hand. Lauren smiled. Gretchen was clearly enamoured with this new friend with his jovial, easy manner, who effortlessly cradled her in his strong arms and spoke to her soothingly. She was being treated like a little princess and loving it!

Lauren followed Josh outside into the small front garden. After the warmth of the cottage, the bitter evening air nipped at their faces as they made their way to Greg's Land Rover. Josh gently lifted Gretchen and placed her on the back seat, covering her with a brightly coloured tartan blanket, then opened the door politely for Lauren.

She noticed a battered silver-grey Subaru Forester on the gravel drive that gently sloped downwards to the single-track lane that led to the village.

'Is that your car?'

'Yes, it used to be Dad's. His new partner drove it before

they bought this one last year. I look after it myself...it might be old but it runs perfectly,' he declared proudly.

'Is your father's partner a vet too?' Lauren made polite conversation while waiting for Greg, gratitude replacing any earlier irritation she had felt towards Josh now she knew Gretchen would be fine.

'Yes, Janelle. She's back at the practice in town, taking clinic today. They work the roster together. When I qualify I'll be able to help them.'

'So, you're at veterinary college?' Lauren inquired.

'I will be. I'm applying to get into uni next year.'

'Good for you! Which one?'

'Exeter is my first choice, but I'll travel further away if I don't get in there. I've got to study hard. I need to get good grades.' He looked earnest. This was obviously important to him.

'You're doing well at college?' she asked.

'Yeah, I'm not doing too badly.'

'Well, that's good. It's a pretty little cottage, peaceful place to study I imagine. Do you live here with your father and Janelle?'

'They live at the Manor and I rent this place. But they're always around if I need them.' He shrugged, in the typically non-committal way of teenage boys. 'It's useful some days, 'cos I get to ask Dad loads of questions and go out with them on visits whenever I like.'

'That's good experience for you.'

The conversation died and Lauren busied herself re-tying her scarf and doing up the top buttons of her coat while they waited for Greg.

'Look, about earlier.' Josh looked awkward. 'I didn't mean for Gretchen to get hurt.'

She turned to him and patted his hand. 'I know you didn't. It was just an accident, luckily no serious harm done and your father came to the rescue.'

'You're not mad then?' For a moment he looked more like a worried boy who'd done something wrong than the brash teenager she'd met on the snow-covered moors. He had been so concerned and helpful and she knew he had done everything he could to put the situation right.

'Of course not,' she reassured him.

Josh looked relieved.

Greg approached at that moment and Charlie bounded over to Josh who caught his collar. 'Come on boy, let's go indoors. Drive safely Dad!' he called and raised his hand in farewell.

Greg settled into the driver's seat. 'OK. Where are we off to?'

'My house is just the other side of the village,' Lauren replied. 'I'll direct you, if you like. Thank you for this.'

'You're welcome. Glad to be of service. The village is so pretty. Is it one of the new houses near the park?'

'Yes, I bought it a few months ago. I grew up nearby, but I'd been living in London for a few years before deciding on a lifestyle change. I've come home.' Inwardly, Lauren winced. He didn't need to know about the painful marriage breakdown after her husbands affair, which had been such a shock to her - although most of their friends seemed to know all about it. Lauren instantly recalled the awful, sinking feeling of despair that had sent her life free-falling into disbelief and chaos. The bitter divorce that inevitably followed had wounded her deeply, shaken her faith in all that she had trusted and eventually led to the decision to come back to her family home, back to those who loved her, in search of peace and solace.

Greg nodded briefly, sensing her reasons for moving touched on some past difficulty for her. 'I know the area. So, do you work in the village?'

'I work in Tavistock. I started my own floristry business a few months ago and I love it! It's actually doing quite well. It's been a lot of hard work, but definitely worth it.'

'How clever. I have no idea about anything artistic. I don't have a creative bone in my body!' he joked, hoping to lift her spirits. It was pride in her achievements that gave her the warm glow she told herself. Not that dazzling smile of his.

Greg's natural warmth and kindly presence made Lauren feel safe and the conversation flowed easily between them. He told her he usually attended farms and worked with large animals, horses being his particular specialty, while Janelle usually ran the clinics and small animal side of the practice. They had a couple of junior assistants visit the practice from time to time to help during their busiest times.

'I'm so glad Gretchen will be all right. I was so worried. How long will it be before she can walk on that leg properly?'

'It *is* sprained, so let her rest for a few days. It could have been much worse.' Greg replied.

'Gosh. So easily done, even though I did ask Josh to be careful. I wish he hadn't thrown the ball quite so many times.'

'I'm sure it was an accident.' Greg looked at her with concern. 'He didn't mean for it to happen.'

Immediately, Lauren wished she could retract her words. She hadn't meant to sound as if she were accusing his son.

'Of course, I realise it was an accident,' she said quickly. 'I just meant I wish it hadn't happened. I mean, well, I asked him not to throw the ball quite so far.'

'If you think it was his fault I'll speak to him. But he's a responsible young man who loves animals and knows how to care for them. I can assure you he was very distressed when he phoned me.'

'Yes, I'm sure he was. I am sorry – I didn't mean it to sound like I blame him.' Lauren bit her sore lip. The mood between them had changed. She could feel it.

The conversation died and she spent the rest of the journey gazing out of the ice-speckled window at the passing scene of the moors, as pretty as any Christmas card. Regretfully, she watched the rolling scene from her window. Areas of the countryside she had known since childhood seemed strangely unfamiliar to her now, enshrouded in a smooth white blanket. Eventually they reached the road that would take them to the village.

'Take a left at the next junction, please,' she directed. 'We're nearly there now.'

The Land Rover crunched up the gravel garden path leading to the front door of her little modern home. A layer of perfect white sugar frosting covered the roses and shrubs either side of them and Greg once again carried the now comfortable Gretchen, wrapped in a cosy blanket and clearly enjoying all the attention and special treatment.

A wave of dry warmth from the central heating hit them as soon as Lauren opened the door. They entered the light, bright hallway and she ushered Greg into the living room, and indicated to an oval wicker basket with a soft pink blanket resting at the foot of the couch.

'Aha!' he smiled. 'This must be madam's bed!' He gently placed Gretchen in her basket.

'Do you play?' he asked, nodding towards the polished walnut upright piano in the corner of the room near large French windows that framed a view of the garden.

'Yes…well, I'm not as proficient as my mother, she's the real pianist.'

'Creativity runs in the family then?'

'I don't know about that.' Lauren removed her knitted cap and ran her fingers through her hair. Should she offer him tea or coffee? 'Thank you so much for everything.'

'Think nothing of it.' His voice was coolly polite. All the earlier warmth and friendliness was missing. *OK, so no tea or coffee.*

'I really didn't mean to accuse Josh,' she said quietly.

Greg looked out of the window. 'I'd better get going. It's not getting any better out there.'

Lauren saw him to the door. 'Thank you again. Please take care. Have a safe journey home.'

She closed the door after him and leaned against it, feeling deflated, exhausted and more than a little annoyed at the situation. She had apologised for implying Greg's son was to blame for Gretchen's injury. What more did he expect? What more could she have done?

Well, what did it matter anyway? She was unlikely to see Greg Harrington again. In future she'd be dealing with her usual vet.

Outside, the drifting white flakes fell bigger and faster.

2

Old Friends

'Well, hello-o-o stranger!' Her sister's voice sang merrily down the phone.

Lauren smiled. She loved her outgoing, cheerful younger sister. Work commitments meant they didn't see as much of each other as they both would like, but Lauren was always pleased to hear from Katie.

Quick, clever and confident, Kate possessed a happy-go-lucky demeanour and an abundance of energy, which more than made up for her slightness of build, or 'petite stature' as their mother would say.

'Hi, Kate, how are you?'

'I'm great! I'm sorry I haven't been in touch for a few weeks. Just working hard as always. How about you?'

'I'm fine. Gretchen had an accident, so we're taking it easy for a week or two.'

'Oh no, Laurie! Is she OK? What happened?'

'She sprained a front leg on our walk the other day. But she's fine – or she will be. We're just resting up and keeping ourselves to ourselves.' Nothing new there. Situation normal. 'What's new with you? Still enjoying your job?'

'Yes, thanks - I love it! It's such a great place to work and we're doing so well. There's talk of another office opening in Plymouth soon. Everyone's so friendly and we all went for drinks on Friday night at that new place off Charles Street to celebrate. James and I are going out again later actually.'

At the mention of James, Lauren rolled her eyes. With her glossy auburn hair and emerald eyes Kate had always unwittingly attracted more than her fair share of male attention. Not that she had ever really noticed any of them. However, recently there had been one new guy in particular; a certain handsome and athletic James Mitchell, supremely self-confident, who was just a little too fond of telling Kate what to do for Lauren's liking.

'He got that promotion he went for, so he's head of the accountancy team now. We're going out in his new car later today with his friends to celebrate.'

'Good news! I'm pleased for you.' Despite her misgivings, Lauren was glad her sister was happy. She could hear the smile in her sister's voice. 'Have a great time.'

'We will! But it will be *even better* when we get together for your birthday next week,' Kate enthused.

'Why? What exactly are *we* doing?' Lauren frowned. She'd made it quite clear she preferred a low-key family gathering to a frivolous party of any kind and had requested no gifts.

'We're having a special day to ourselves. Honestly, Laurie, you didn't think I'd let your birthday slip by, did you?' Kate laughed. 'I have a few tricks up my sleeve for the morning then I'm treating you to lunch!'

'Hmm…' She might have known her sister would have it

all worked out in fine detail.

'Oh, come on, Laurie,' Kate cajoled. 'You knew I would do something special for your birthday – it's not every day you turn thirty. Remember, we're here for a *good* time, not a *long* time!' Lauren could hear her smiling as she sang down the phone. 'Besides, it'll be *fun!* Remember that?'

'OK, just tell me where and when.' Lauren resigned herself to her fate, which apparently lay in her sister's hands. Heaven help her.

'Great! I'll pick you up at nine. Don't keep me waiting – we have appointments at Volare at ten. Love you! Bye-ee!'

Lauren opened her mouth to protest but Kate had already hung up. Volare was an exclusive spa in the city centre, and combined with lunch this would cost her sister a small fortune. Kate had seriously overstepped the mark here. However, she didn't have time to dwell on the situation for long as the trill of her mobile cut through her anxiety and Julia, her assistant, quizzed her about a delivery for the next day. With mixed feelings of irritation and excitement Lauren curled up on the couch with her tea and flicked through the channels of the television until she found a film she liked the look of for the evening.

* * *

The next morning, Lauren carefully manoeuvred her car through the grey slush along Tavistock's busy main street and turned into the narrow lane that led to the rear of her shop. As she parked opposite the sign, *Parking for Heaven Scent Customers ONLY*, she smiled at the name. It had been Kate's clever idea of course, and at first she'd had reservations; but the name had grown on her. It suited the stylishly chic atmosphere of the bright, modern shop the sisters had designed together and seemed memorable for the customers.

Lauren opened the back door of her cobalt blue VW Golf, waiting as Gretchen carefully lowered herself onto the pavement, her foreleg still a little stiff but still excited at being out for an afternoon adventure. It was cold but no longer freezing and although it had stopped snowing at last, there was still a crisp edge to the air. The sky was bright azure and the frozen town shimmered in a weak, silvery sunlight, making the wet pavement and walls feel hard, as if they had been coated in steel.

A pretty girl with tight blonde curls cut into a fashionable bob looked up from the pile of cuttings strewn over the counter she was working on when Lauren entered the shop. Twenty-two-year-old Julia Adams was cheerful and enthusiastic and loved working at Heaven Scent. She had the kind of warm hazel eyes that always seemed to be smiling. Her gentle, patient manner was popular with the customers and as she lived locally she knew all the regular clients. Lauren had warmed to Julia from the start and was grateful to have found such a reliable assistant whose natural sense of style produced fresh and stunningly original ideas for their customers each week. They ran the shop together while Julia's boyfriend Craig Michaels attended to most of their deliveries in the afternoons after working mornings at a large hardware store across town.

'There, all done!' Julia exclaimed proudly while tying a silver ribbon into an elaborate bow with a flourish. 'The finishing touch for the Tavistock Hotel's arrangement.'

Behind her, Lauren spied a splendid spherical gold and white creation. Sunshine yellow chrysanthemums were separated by elegant lemon tea roses and white carnations, with perfect, tiny Lily of the Valley bells scattered throughout like sugar sprinkles. The edges softened by gypsophila, weaving an intricate white lace around the entire creation. Lauren nodded in approval; the local hotel was an important regular client and she was sure this arrangement would look stunning on their front desk.

'Look what came in this morning,' Julia enthused, producing an array of Cymbidium orchids Lauren had ordered especially for the weekend.

Their pastel-coloured petals were so delicate they could have been made of spun sugar. They would be perfect for a wedding bouquet she had already designed and Julia would make tomorrow.

'Gorgeous, aren't they?'

'They most certainly are,' Lauren smiled. She knew her assistant would confidently handle the regular orders. 'I'll draw a plan and leave it out for you for tomorrow. We still have some of that silver ribbon I think – is that OK?'

'Sure, no problem,' Julia reassured her, reaching for her handbag with one hand and sliding the other into her jacket. 'It's a family dinner tonight. I'd better go, or I'll be late.' She cast a glance at Craig waiting for her outside the shop. 'I promised Mum we'd collect a few things on the way home. I'll call if I need you.'

'OK, well, off you go!' Lauren handed her friend a colourful mixed bouquet for her mother. Don't be late. Have a good time!' Julia grinned and waved as she darted through the door.

After serving a few customers, Lauren settled into making individual arrangements for gifts. She loved the goblet-shaped Calla lilies; their perfect, even-coloured petals complemented the slim coloured glass vases, which sparkled in the golden afternoon light streaming in from the shop window.

She was so lucky to be spoiled for choice; the lilies were every colour from purest white and delicate shell pink to scarlet blood red; pale lemon through to russet gold; light cream to the deepest royal purple. She loved her work and became so absorbed that the time seemed to melt away until the trill of the shop phone broke her concentration.

'Good afternoon, Heaven Scent – how may I help you?'

'Hello, I'd like to place an order please.' A man's voice. Deep, sexy. *Familiar.* Why familiar? Lauren's mind momentarily spun with confusion.

Of course. Greg Harrington.

'I need a special bouquet to be delivered next Saturday.'

'Hello, Greg. It's Lauren Sinclair here. How are you?'

A pause.

'Fine, thank you.' His tone was clipped, polite. 'It's Janelle's birthday soon. I'd like something exceptional for her, please.'

'Naturally, I'd be glad to help.' Lauren forced her tone to remain neutral and efficient. The gorgeous Janelle. She remembered the photograph with a twinge of envy. Well, whatever she came up with, it would have to be absolutely stunning to befit someone so beautiful. At once, Lauren pushed any jealousy to the back of her mind and started thinking professionally. What would he like to present her with? What would be suitable for his partner's special day?

'What are her favourites? I can put together a lovely mixed bouquet. Do you know what colours she likes? I will have some superb deep red roses on order very soon, which may suit you.'

'No, not red. Perhaps…pink.'

'No problem, we can make up something special in pink tones and have it delivered for you.' Lauren noted the order in her appointments book and carefully took down the delivery details. Not red roses, she noted with surprise. Most men liked those for their partners. Maybe he would buy her some for Valentine's Day. Well, now he'd found Heaven Scent, he'd know where to come.

Lauren finished the Calla lily gift boxes and started designing Janelle's bouquet. Her mind was full of ideas – he'd asked for something *exceptional*. That would mean pushing the boundaries a little. Something a little…unexpected. Unique. Inspired by the challenge, Lauren was surprised she was so determined to impress Greg. Somehow it was important to her.

After a few hours of steadily working she sat back in her chair and stretched. Coffee! That's what was needed now. She headed to the kitchenette at the back of the shop and absentmindedly flicked through the local paper as she waited for the kettle to boil. One colourful advertisement bedecked in red hearts and roses among the grey print caught her attention. The Lions Cub Valentine's Ball was to be held at the town hall next month. Tickets would be on sale soon. Lauren made a mental note to order extra red roses and ribbons.

She had almost finished drawing up the plans for Greg's bouquet and the bridal order she had promised Julia when the shop doorbell tinkled. Glancing up, she grinned in delight.

'Hi, sweetie!' Elaine Davies was Lauren's oldest friend. Average build with neat, short dark hair and a pretty smile, she reached to give Lauren a hug. 'I was just passing on the way to the shops and thought I'd look in – how's things?'

'Good! Lovely to see you!' Lauren beamed. She and

Elaine had been best friends since school. They had shared secrets, jokes and ambitions until eventually Lauren had gone to London and Elaine had married her high school sweetheart. Dependable, capable and kind, Elaine had become an excellent cook and housewife. She had supported her family by working as a registered nurse at the local hospital while her husband Paul had started his own business as an electrician; now she was a stay-at-home mother to their son. Golden haired three-year-old Matthew cheekily peeped around his mother's legs and squealed in delight as Gretchen approached her little friend to say hello.

'I was saying to Paul this morning you should come to dinner one evening next week, if you're free. Oh, and this is for your birthday...' Elaine handed her a prettily decorated box of handmade truffles with a violet envelope. 'A little something especially for you.'

'Aw, thank you! You shouldn't have.'

'Nonsense! You knew we wouldn't forget your birthday.' Elaine laughed. 'It's your special day. You must spoil yourself. Now I'd better get this little man home. Say goodbye to Gretchen, Mattie.' She took his hand and led him to the door, where she turned back to Lauren. 'Don't forget to give me a ring and let me know when you can come to dinner, OK?'

Lauren smiled. 'Thank you. I will.'

At five o'clock Lauren switched off the lights and locked the shop door. Cool air swirled around her and her breath streamed in front of her as she walked to her car with Gretchen close at her heels. The evening was already closing in around her, and along the street shop lights spilled golden light onto the dark, shiny wet pavement. She was looking forward to a peaceful evening with her mother at her house on the edge of Dartmoor; Shirley had agreed to take Gretchen for the day while she and Kate were in town. Lauren had missed her mother over the New Year celebrations - she had been away visiting a friend in the New Forrest - and she welcomed the serene warmth an evening in the place she truly thought of as 'home' conjured inside her.

* * *

Lauren couldn't help a contented smile as she drove along the unlit country lane towards the village. Spending time with her mother always made her feel relaxed and inspired; Shirley was as strong and stoical as their sturdily built, stone clad Edwardian family home and had been the backbone of their family since her father had passed away suddenly from a heart attack ten years ago.

As her car wound its way steadily uphill Lauren could see the familiar golden windows glowing in the distance through wintry gloom. The house, standing alone on the edge of the moors, radiated warmth and homeliness filling her with a sense of peace. Lauren always marvelled at the sight. Named 'Sherian' – a composition of both parents' names - Shirley's impeccable taste in décor had ensured an exceptionally high standard to the finish. Lauren knew there was no question of her mother ever moving away. She loved Sherian too much to ever leave, it was as if her heart and soul were entwined with the place. Lauren completely understood.

The beautiful old grey stone and slate-tiled house drew closer into view and Lauren turned and drove slowly up the driveway. The garden was cheerful even in the midst of winter, with holly laden with berries, yellow jasmine and flashes of purple and white heather, thanks to her mother's talent for gardening. Polyanthus and cyclamen dotted about in baskets and pots were scattered around the house like bright paint spatters against the snow.

Stepping out of her car, Lauren could hear piano music drifting serenely over the garden towards her. Anyone else would assume the music was a CD, but Lauren knew better. The music stopped, and a few moments later Shirley opened the door, arms wide in greeting, her trim figure a silhouette against the warm yellow light from the hallway. Two little cocker spaniels streamed out of the doorway, like rockets of energy, their tails a blur as they scampered first to Lauren, then to Gretchen and back to Lauren again in a frenzy of pure excitement. Golden Chester and pretty, plump little black and grey Grace were her Mothers' cheeky but beloved companions of many years.

'*Welcome home,* darling!' Shirley hugged her older daughter and kissed her cheek. 'Come in out of the cold. Are you hungry? I made soup and strudel – Grace, come back here. Chester, do *shut up!'*

The three dogs streaked joyfully ahead and Lauren gratefully followed her mother indoors, into the comfort of warmth and the sweet aroma of baking, suddenly aware that she really was very hungry. She marvelled again at the ornate detail that surrounded her in the beautifully baroque hallway. Her parents had painstakingly restored the old house with love and care during the early years of their marriage and it had been the heartfelt centre of their world ever since.

Twisting the brass handle of the great oak-panelled door, Lauren took a step inside and drew a breath, enjoying the familiar scent of pine - scented polish and baking. Above the dining table, a mini chandelier dripped with strings of crystal prisms, making tiny rainbows of colour against the bright light. A warmth of gladness to be back among the beautifully charming and familiar surroundings she loved engulfed her.

After a sumptuous dinner of homemade vegetable soup and apple strudel with cream, she and her mother settled down to chat together in the tastefully decorated lounge at the back of the house. The polished wooden floorboards gave way to a thick pastel-grey carpet. Deep blue velvet curtains drawn across the large French doors shut out the night. At the opposite end of the room a large creamy marble fireplace speckled with an intricate web of delicate blue veins emitted heat from it's burning coals, which shimmered deep red and glowed like large rubies behind the impressive hearth. A small silver-grey tabby cat stretched luxuriously on the rug before the hearth, then jumped up and onto Shirley's lap as she settled on the couch.

'And who's this?' Lauren reached over to tickle the newcomer under her chin. The little tabby began to purr contentedly.

'Tabitha. One of the shopkeepers in the village found her wandering in the snow last week. No one seemed to know where she'd come from and she was starving. Well, we couldn't have that, could we, my sweet.' Shirley smoothed a brown speckled hand gently over Tabitha's back.

Lauren smiled. Underneath that tough exterior her mother had a tender heart. Especially where needy animals were concerned.

'I took her along to the vet to be checked over. I went to the Harrington practice at the other side of the village because it was quicker, although I don't usually go there. I usually travel to John Gendell's practice in Tavistock. Have done for years. He always has Chester's favourite biscuits.'

Mention of the Harrington vet surgery prompted Lauren to recount the incident on the moors.

'Poor Gretchen,' said Shirley. 'That must have been awful for her.'

Gretchen twitched her ears and raised her head at the mention of her name. Shirley leaned over and smoothed the fur on her head. 'At least the lad helped you. I haven't met him, but I will say Gregory Harrington seems very nice and runs a good practice. He was so patient with Tabitha. I dare say he deserves his success, especially after losing his wife to cancer a few years ago – it can't have been easy for him or his lad.'

That explained why Josh had not mentioned his mother. Lauren felt a stab of sadness at what Greg and Josh had gone through; it must have been incredibly tough for both of them. She knew how heart-wrenchingly awful it was to lose a parent at a young age and couldn't help reflecting on her own loss. Her gaze fell on her father's photograph on the mantel. His gentle smile reached out to her, dressed in his best suit and about to receive an award for his successful accountancy business.

'He would have been so proud of you.' Shirley's quietly spoken words interrupted Lauren's thoughts. 'He always believed in you and loved you both so much.'

'I know.'

Brian had been a contemplative, kind man with a great deal of patience who considered all options in life carefully, in contrast to the lively, vivacious extrovert he had married. They had complemented one another perfectly and enjoyed a happy marriage until fate dealt them a dreadful blow. One afternoon, he had finished helping Kate with a maths problem and had decided to work in the garden. Shirley had watched helplessly from the window as he'd stumbled and collapsed. Suddenly, he was gone. It had hit them all hard, but her mother had been devastated. Brian had been the true love of Shirley's life and it was as if part of her soul had been torn away.

Lauren folded her mother's hands in hers.

'How's Kate, Mum?' Lauren asked to brighten the mood. 'I haven't seen her in a while, although she phoned earlier and told me about a new opportunity she's been given at work. She seems happy, but I'm just not sure about this James she's so fond of.'

'Well, I can't say I am very impressed with his attitude to her at times.' A frown crossed Shirley's brow. 'He's a bit too big for his boots for my liking. I think he likes to tell her what to do too often, if you ask me.'

'She's so soft, Mum, she'd give anyone the benefit of the doubt.'

'Yes, well, if he bullies her I'm afraid I'll be tempted to tell him what I think, make no mistake! But until then, I am prepared to keep quiet and give him a chance because she does seem to like him.'

Lauren nodded. 'Yes, that's how I feel too.'

'And how are you these days?' Shirley asked with genuine concern. 'Glad to be home? Not missing London too much?'

'Not at all.' Lauren spoke quietly, with conviction. 'It's been a relief to come back, and the shop has kept me so busy I haven't had time to think about what happened.'

'That's good. I know it was all so upsetting. A dreadful shock. I am always here if you need to talk to me about anything, darling, you know that. You've been very brave, but you needn't lock yourself away from life. Never think you have to cope entirely on your own.'

'I'm fine thanks, Mum. Really I am.' It wasn't too far from the truth. She was 'fine'. Not great, not deeply happy. Heaven Scent kept her busy by day and she felt happy enough with her music, books and films in the solitude of her little house in the evenings. Of course, there was also her beloved Gretchen. The quiet, simple life suited her 'just fine'. At least, that's what she told herself.

'The shop has really taken off now and Julia has really excelled herself this week with the hotel's order. I've decided let her do a wedding by herself.'

'Well, that's great news, darling. I'm so proud of you. You've done so well.' She studied Lauren thoughtfully. 'But… how about *you?* Since your divorce it's as if you're afraid to live, shut up on your own in the house each evening and weekend. Are you happy here? I do *so* want you to be happy.'

'Oh, Mum! Of course I am! I love being here with you and Katie. I just need some time I suppose, after the breakup. I don't really feel like taking any chances and sometimes I think it might be better if I stay on my own. Far less complicated. Besides, I'm not alone. I have Gretchen.'

'Yes, I know. I'm only saying that history needn't be a trap. It *is* possible to shake off the weight of old troubles and pain. Don't let past misfortunes shape your future, my dear. Time and tide wait for no man – go out, meet people… enjoy your life!'

'I'm not about to make the same mistakes.' Lauren spoke softly. 'I don't want to find myself having to face all that grief again, Mum.'

'You should never make such assumptions; you don't

know what life might have in store for you. One day, your life will exceed your expectations. You'll see!'

Lauren smiled. She knew her mother meant well. So did her friends when they told her the same thing. But she wasn't convinced they were right.

'Besides,' Lauren said as she idly flicked through a glossy Theatre Royal brochure, 'I quite like my own company. I'm comfortable in my own home. Oh! *Carmen....*' A colourful image exploding across the centre pages of the brochure caught her attention. 'How spectacular! I would *love* to see it. Oh, it's showing here next week...'

'I know – I tried to get tickets for your birthday but they'd sold out – I didn't realise it was showing here because I've been away.'

'Never mind, Mum, there will be another time.' Shirley got up from her armchair and crossed the lounge to a large oak dresser.

'I understand Kate has a busy day planned for you tomorrow,' she smiled, 'so I may not see you until after your big day. You'd better have your birthday present now. I couldn't get the tickets, so this will have to do.' Shirley produced a rectangular gift box, wrapped in colourful paper.

'Mum, I said no presents!' Lauren rolled her eyes in protest, but smiled at her mother.

'Oh, go on, my girl. What's a birthday without a gift? Well, aren't you going to open it?'

'It's not *actually* my birthday yet,' Lauren observed, glancing at the clock on the mantel.

'Only another ninety minutes to go. Besides, I want to see if you like it.'

Lauren opened one end of the paper to reveal the edge of

an antique faded navy velvet case edged in gold. As it slid out of the paper, Lauren felt it had a familiar feel to it. The ornate clasp was of good quality and opened with a snap. Nestled inside on midnight blue silk, a delicate sapphire and diamond choker twinkled up at her with two tastefully matching drop earrings either side.

Lauren gasped and then felt her eyes fill with tears that threatened to spill onto her cheeks. She recognised these old friends. She had seen them many times before and clearly remembered them from her childhood. They had been her grandmother's most precious possessions. As a child she had only been allowed to look at them when her mother was around; but when her mother had gone out and Granny was in charge, she had been allowed to wear them.

'Well, would you like them? Do you remember them?' her mother peered at her anxiously. "I didn't mean to upset you."

'Yes,' Lauren finally managed to say. 'I do remember them. Thank you, Mum. It's the *best* gift… it's perfect.'

'Good. That's all right then.' Shirley hugged her daughter close. 'I wanted you to have them. You always loved them as a child. Have a super day tomorrow, darling.'

'I will,' Lauren assured her, though she felt less confident of the outcome than she sounded. Katie's ideas of a super birthday were so different from her own.

3

Celebrations

Lauren and Gretchen woke early after a restless night filled with anticipation. Glancing out of the window into the pale dawn light Lauren saw a fine mist slowly lifting, the grass still glistening with dew. By half past eight, she was quietly nursing her second cup of coffee, nervously wondering what the day ahead would bring. At 9 a.m. sharp, Kate's bright red new Fiesta STi pulled up in her drive and Lauren met her sister at the door.

'Happy birthday! I've been *so* looking forward to this. Are you *actually ready*?' Kate teased as Lauren grabbed her purse and handbag. 'No last minute excuses?'

'Let's go, before I think of something.'

They reached Plymouth in good time despite the morning traffic. Soft white lighting and delicious vanilla scent enveloped them as they entered Volare and quiet piano music drifted towards them. Slim figures clad in white jeans and T-shirts glided soundlessly through different doors. An attractive blonde with diamond white smile, hair pulled back into a sleek ponytail and a badge with 'Suzanne' emblazoned on her chest approached the sisters.

Kate whispered to the receptionist and Suzanne ushered them into the salon.

Three hours later Lauren stepped out of the salon feeling she had been thoroughly pampered and polished from head to toe. There was no doubt she had enjoyed herself immensely and she *was* grateful to Kate but she felt it had been far too generous. Of course, Kate dismissively waved away her complaints.

'It's been too long since we had a chance to do anything together. Besides, I can *afford* to treat you now, and I couldn't before...and you look great!'

Lauren did like her pale pink nails and the sleek, shiny new hairstyle that swung about her shoulders. Suzanne had known exactly what would suit her.

'Right, on to Bustopher's!' Kate skipped excitedly by her side.

Lauren stopped and stared at her. The swish new wine bar had received rave reviews from the local media. Reservations were almost impossible to get; Kate must have booked weeks ago.

'Bustopher *Jones*? Are you serious?' There seemed to be no end to her surprises today.

'Yep! You betcha! I've been *dying* to go...aw, come on Laurie, don't be a spoilsport!' Kate wheedled.

With a sigh of resignation, Lauren reluctantly allowed herself to be led to the city's most stylish venue.

A wave of warmth, chatter and upbeat music hit them as Kate pushed open the large glass door of the sophisticated bar. Now and then laughter broke through the background hum. The scene had an understated sparkle about it. Crystal glasses captured the light on the pristine tables, and an ocean blue feature wall with silver sail - shaped sculptures was a sharp contrast to simple white walls and chrome and white furnishings. Groups of people gathered at the bar and clustered around tables and the place was extremely busy with a vibrant upbeat atmosphere.

Kate grinned at her sister, clearly happy to be among the city's most fashionable and chic. A waiter approached them in an attentive but not overbearing manner and they were whisked to a small table near a window overlooking a modern stone sculptured water feature. He produced two smart gold-edged leather-bound menus with a flourish and they studied the impressive selection on offer. Kate ordered a glass of Chablis for Lauren and Perrier for herself because she was driving.

Lauren had to admit the food was exquisite and beautifully prepared. Her scallops with simple green salad were so elegantly presented and Kate's crab cakes with chive and roast tomato salsa were almost a work of art. Kate had gone to such great lengths to give her a splendid day out that Lauren decided she may as well relax and allow herself to enjoy it. Towards the end of the meal a waiter approached their table and discreetly produced an open bottle of Billecart-Salmon rose champagne in ice and two crystal flutes. Shocked, Lauren stared at her sister. Had Kate taken leave of her senses? This was *way* too much. She opened her mouth to protest, but Kate's giggles interrupted. She was looking over her shoulder, towards the far side of the restaurant.

Lauren followed her gaze across the floor and her eyes rested on a tanned, blond man leaning nonchalantly against the bar, his handsome smile directly confidently at her. Lauren just had time to catch her breath before he moved away from the bar, his movement fluid and mesmerising. She could hardly tear her gaze away from him as he drew closer. He was heading towards her!

'Erik!' Kate sang out joyfully and signalled for him to join them. 'This is my sister, Lauren. Let me introduce Erik Danielsen.'

'Ah, yes! Kate's beautiful sister, the birthday girl. Lovely to meet you.' He flashed her another perfect white smile. She smiled politely in return, trying not to stare in wonder at the piercing clarity of his sapphire eyes. Good-looking with a lean, athletic build and clad in a soft grey Armani suit. Yes, this must be Kate's boss, the most eligible and infamous bachelor in the south west of England. She had heard the enthusiastic way Kate and her friends talked about him but until now had dismissed their hype as schoolgirl nonsense. With Erik standing in front of her, she could clearly see the reason for their speculation. He was amazing.

Lauren's mind whirled as she desperately tried to recall all she had heard about him – especially as he seemed to know about her. Erik Danielsen, thirty-five, head of the prestigious international insurance company Clarence and Fulton. An exceptionally sharp businessman and top earning insurance agent, his skill and dedication had made him famous among the elite in the business world, and his impeccable sense of justice and skilful leadership made him hugely popular with his team. Under his direction, the company had recently expanded to include offices in Plymouth, Exeter, Bristol, London, New York and Paris.

An expert snow-boarder, his parents were Scandinavian

and he spoke fluent Norwegian, Swedish, Danish and English. Last week he'd returned from competing in a winter sports championship in Switzerland – that would explain the tan. Wealthy. Single. *Dangerous*, her subconscious added. Lauren coolly returned his gaze and extended her hand in what she hoped was a sophisticated manner, but felt herself inwardly blushing and desperately tried not to let it show.

'Likewise,' she responded, and wondered whether this was indeed a chance meeting of if Kate had set her up. And what else had Kate told him about her aside from the fact it was her birthday?

His smooth bronzed hand lightly folded over her own.

'I hope you don't mind the champagne…I couldn't resist wishing you a happy birthday.'

'Hi!' breezed over to Kate. Lauren tore her gaze from Erik in time to see James quickly lean over and kiss Kate on the cheek. 'Had a good morning?' he asked, taking a sip of her drink and helping himself to the last forkful of crab cake.

Erik nodded in the direction of three smartly dressed figures at the end of the bar.

'OK, James, clients await. Time to go. It was very nice to meet you, Lauren. We'll see you later. Enjoy!'

Lauren watched their retreating backs mingle into the crowd, suddenly aware she hadn't had a chance to thank him for the champagne.

'Kate!' Lauren hissed accusingly. 'You *knew* they were going to be here. Why didn't you tell me we were going to meet them? And what did he mean – see us *later*?'

'OK, OK! Take a breath.' Kate rolled her eyes in mock frustration. 'Don't panic. I s'pose I'd better explain.' She grinned. 'Maria – that's Erik's personal assistant – needed a smart venue for a meeting with some important clients today and I happened to mention that I wanted to book somewhere nice for your birthday. I guess she thought it was an appropriate place for both occasions.' Kate shrugged. 'I wouldn't have got a table here if it hadn't been booked by Maria in Erik's name. Besides, I wasn't one hundred per cent sure they'd still be here when we arrived…although I knew there was a good chance.'

So *that's* how Kate had managed to get a table here. She had Erik to thank. 'Erik's a nice guy, and when he found out it was your birthday he wanted to do something. There's a staff party at Chansons wine bar tonight to celebrate exceeding our quota over the last six months – and I *may* have mentioned we would be there.' Kate looked up at her sister through lowered eyelashes. 'I really should go anyway, and Erik said he'd like to meet you…' She trailed off.

'You should have told me.' 'I might have been busy or…'

Kate gave her a 'yeah-*that*-was-likely' look. She knew too well that Lauren's important date would be with Jane Austen and a mug of cocoa.

'Anyway,' said Lauren, 'what do you mean he wanted to meet me? Kate, what have you *done*?'

'Nothing!' she insisted. 'Well…nothing *bad*. He is just a nice guy, has a lot of friends and wanted to do something special when he found out it was your birthday…and you'll be *completely spoiled* – I *know* you will!'

Lauren glared at her. Had she taken leave of her senses? This couldn't be happening. Her incorrigible little sister had set her up on a date with *Erik Danielsen*. She would be the centre of attention if she went with him – not something she was either used to or comfortable with. Lauren could well imagine Erik's type – he had a lot of female attention and he may well be a 'nice guy' and the life and soul of the party, but she doubted she could trust him.

She hated being set up on a date – it smacked of pathetic; she was dull compared to shining, social butterfly Kate. The boring, home-alone sister with the empty diary. She liked the quiet life. It suited her fine. Why did everyone else take such exception to her lifestyle choice?

'Oh come on, Laurie, I didn't mean to upset you. Besides, it'll be a great evening and I *really would* like you to come – but I knew you would never agree to coming on your own with just me. Now there'll be four of us.' She smiled in satisfaction.

The knot in Lauren's stomach tightened. Throughout the thirty-minute car journey home over the moorland highway, Kate chattered brightly, trying to keep the atmosphere light and cheery. Lauren sat in virtual silence, only half listening while her mind anxiously contemplated the evening ahead. As they approached her house, she cheered a little. Perhaps Kate was right... It would be nice to have an evening out with her sister, and really, how bad could it *be*?

* * *

Lauren nervously glanced at her bedside clock as she deftly flicked through the clothes hanging in her wardrobe. The taxi was due at seven so she didn't have long to get ready. On the bright side, at least she had no time to panic. By the time she and Kate had returned home it was almost evening and getting dark. Lauren had made some tea, checked her messages, called Julia at the shop and called her mother to receive copious birthday wishes and make sure Gretchen was behaving herself. A bubble bath and glass of wine later she was draped in a fluffy bath towel in front of her wardrobe, pondering the dilemma of what to wear.

As she rifled through her wardrobe her stomach tied itself in knots. Had this been three or four years ago in London she would have had no trouble dressing up and going out, even enjoyed the anticipation of a night on the town. Now she was feeling distinctly anxious at the thought of spending an evening with *Erik.*

'Right, that's it.' Lauren decisively grabbed a hanger with an expensive, sleek designer dress she knew showed off her curvy figure perfectly. She was no supermodel, but she did know how to make the best of what she had. Silver heels lengthened her legs, shimmering in sheer gossamer stockings, and her pearls complimented the creaminess of her skin and completed her classic style.

One last glance at the hallway mirror and another quick coat of shiny pale rose lipstick and she was out the door into the waiting taxi.

* * *

'Lauren!' Kate shrieked as she entered the brightly lit, vibrant club.

The darkened venue pulsated with life as Lauren took a moment to get her bearings. Feeling extremely self-conscious, she took a deep breath and forced herself to step into the crowd, the overhead spotlight illuminating her from head to toe in the midst of the most popular bar in town. Kate bounced through the crowd, red hair shining in the lights. Lauren relaxed a little. No one would be watching her now her vivacious sister had joined her. She marvelled at how Kate was completely at home with fashionable high society; being the centre of attention had never bothered her. By comparison Lauren found this sort of encounter daunting, *intimidating* even. Kate's presence gave her courage and she allowed herself to be ushered to the bar past a group of beautiful, immaculately dressed girls who watched them carefully as they walked. A glass of champagne was promptly produced and pushed into her hand. One of the girls turned and openly stared at her before turning back to her party.

'Come this way, we've been waiting for you…Ooh! Don't you look simply *divine!*' Kate swayed towards her, dressed in a 1950s dress that showed off her trim figure impeccably, her back swathed in sheer lace. She could fall into a muddy ditch and come up looking like a film star, Lauren thought ruefully. Kate grabbed her hand and announced to the table of elegant strangers who were enquiringly gazing at her, 'Everyone, this is my sister Lauren. It's her *birthday!*'

Exuberant cheers and birthday wishes erupted and Erik appeared beside her with that gorgeous smile. He lightly touched her arm. 'Happy birthday, Lauren,' he whispered.

Lauren suddenly felt the need to sit down, unsure whether it was to be less conspicuous or because she suddenly felt vaguely dizzy.

She positioned herself as elegantly as she could into a space made for her, aware a woman with glasses and mousy brown hair was watching her studiously across the table. Without taking her eyes off Lauren she leaned in and whispered to the woman sitting next to her. The woman whipped her head around and stared unapologetically, taking in every detail. Uncomfortable under their scrutiny, Lauren quickly looked away and leaned in to join the conversation with Kate and her friends. What did those girls matter? She would enjoy herself tonight.

Slowly, with great deliberation, the woman unfurled from her seat and stood before her. The sight was astounding. All the men in the room seemed to agree, their eyes involuntarily drawn to this vision of glamorous perfection. Tall and slim with flawless golden skin and clad in an expensive backless dress that seemed to magically cling to the curves of her toned figure, her shiny dark hair swung across her face like a curtain as she leaned to talk to her friend. As if on command, the woman with the glasses stood and the two of them turned and walked towards the bar.

Erik interrupted Lauren's thoughts.

'Thank you for coming. I was delighted when Kate said you'd be here.'

'Thank you for inviting me – I hope I'm not gate-crashing your celebration.'

He returned her smile with another dazzling starburst that made her heart jump. 'Not at all! Would you like a drink?'

His eyes fixed on hers and heat flooded to her cheeks. She managed a mumbled, 'Yes, please,' and almost had to tear herself away from his gaze to the glass of Moet he gave her.

Dammit…he's amazing!

'Kate tells me you have your own little business. Boutique or something, isn't it?'

Lauren felt a pang of indignation. He'd sounded a little patronising.

Maybe he's just trying to be polite. 'I have a small florist shop in the centre of Tavistock.'

'Very nice! So, tell me, what are your favourite flowers?'

'Hmm…I love Calla lilies for their delicacy. And roses for their perfection.'

'Yes, very... elegant,' he mused, looking directly at her. Lauren felt as if his deep blue eyes could see right through her very soul. Was he this charming to all the women here? She was certain he would be.

Lauren was introduced to Erik's team and found them surprisingly easy company. She soon felt herself relax and able to join the conversation. Erik was sociable and gracious, mixing with his staff and many personal friends, attentively returning to her to fill her glass or ask if she was OK, which made her feel special. Kate made her laugh with a few jokes and observations before trying to get her to 'hit the dance floor' with James and her friends. Lauren laughed but refused; she was not quite confident enough to make a spectacle of herself by dancing. She envied her younger sister's easy confidence and natural grace.

'Who were those two women sitting across the table from us?' Lauren asked Kate as soon as she had a chance.

'Oh, them. Clara Beaufort and Cynthia Martell. Clara is Erik's second in command, and she's one tough, smart cookie. Erik says she's a perfectionist. Everyone else is scared stiff of her!' Kate laughed. 'She's Cynthia's friend at the office. I really don't know Cynthia very well because she's only just joined the sales team. I *do* know I wouldn't want to cross Clara, though, that's for sure.' Kate dropped her voice and leaned closer to Lauren. 'They say every one of the rival candidates for the second in charge position were fired a few weeks after Clara got the job. Seriously, I really *wouldn't* want to upset her.'

Erik took a seat beside Lauren during the evening, eloquently answering her questions about his work and how the insurance world worked. 'Look at it this way. Most people do not know what they want. Freedom of choice is what we all want; but freedom *from* choice is what we need. Sure, it's great to have choices, to be informed and be able to give consent to something we agree with or aspire to; but after a while too many choices can be overwhelming, even frightening. That's what my fantastic team at Clarence and Fulton does: narrow those choices and rise to the challenge of providing the perfect options for our clients. We attend to those all-important details and offer individually tailor-made policies that are so appealing to our clients they often just can't refuse. We offer the best. We *are* the best! My team are great people, and we are bloody good at what we do.'

Lauren nodded. She could feel the pride and integrity in his words.

Towards the end of the evening, the music slowed and Lauren was feeling mellow as the champagne worked its magic. She had enjoyed herself, met new and interesting people and really had not seen so much of Erik after all. He was much in demand, very popular. Obviously he had far better things to do than stay with her all evening. Her relief was laced with disappointment that she had not seen as much of this powerful, intriguing and utterly gorgeous man as she had thought she might.

Like magic Erik appeared before her, his hand extended. 'Dance?' he asked.

Lauren could think of a thousand reasons why not - having two left feet, a limited knowledge of any formal dance steps and being too shy sprang to mind - but such trivialities were clearly not acceptable to Erik, who took her by the hand and confidently drew her towards him. He led her to a space on the floor and placed a hand gently but firmly on her waist.

'I'm sorry. I haven't spent as much time with you as I would have liked. There are a lot of people here I felt duty-bound to speak to.' He smiled at Lauren and the air surrounding her suddenly felt tangible with magic.

'Not at all,' she replied, finding it easy to relax and fall into step with him. 'I've enjoyed myself immensely. Thank you for a perfectly lovely evening.'

'My pleasure' he replied, drawing her irresistibly closer to him, his breath warm and inviting on her neck. Lauren smiled back, her body now tethered to his magnetic pull and finding herself lingering between two worlds, the tangible and the surreal, spellbound.

She could feel her heart beating, and the air around her seemed thicker, softer, and protective somehow. No use fighting, she decided. This was one situation where being stoic and sensible was no good.

She allowed herself to melt in his arms, everything around them fading until there seemed only the two of them left in the world, and nothing and no one else seemed to matter.

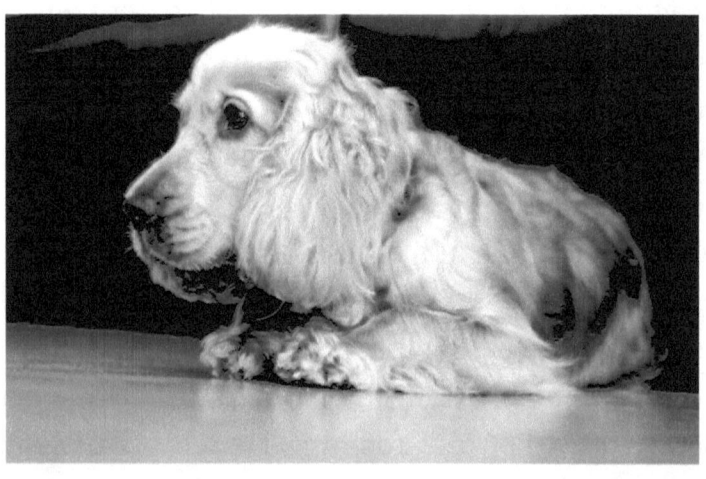

4

Angels

The next day Lauren woke late, sunlight steaming through her window. As she sat up and looked at her clock she heard the thump, thump of Gretchen's' tail on the floor next to her bed. Memories of the previous night hazily drifted back to her and Lauren realised she had thoroughly enjoyed herself. Erik had been kind and attentive and had made her feel so welcome, but she was sure he was just being polite. After all, he had been equally charming to all the ladies at the club.

Lauren headed for the bathroom, pushing wayward strands of hair out of her eyes. She caught a glimpse of herself in the bathroom mirror, tousled hair and pale faced with no makeup. Erik had just been polite to her, nothing more. He had his pick of far more glamorous women, slimmer and much prettier than her. With a shrug and a hint of regret Lauren stepped under the warm steam of her shower. *Whatever.* She'd had a good time. Time now to get a move on. The morning was slipping away and she and Gretchen had to look lively if they were going to make it to Sunday lunch at her mother's house.

An hour later Lauren's blue Golf slowed to a stop outside Sherian next to her sister's sports car. The golden glow from the open doorway reached out to her as she walked up the path armed with her handbag and a bottle of Chablis in one hand and Gretchen's' lead in the other. The smell of roast lamb drifted alluringly towards them.

'Hi!' Kate smiled up at her sister from the kitchen table where she was attempting to chop vegetables.

Lauren grinned at her younger sister. Kate had never been at home in the kitchen. 'Want a hand with that?'

'Sure, thanks. You know what a domestic goddess I am!'

Kate grinned and Lauren rolled her eyes.

'We want to eat *this* week, not next month,' she retorted and took the sharp knife safely from her sister's hand. 'Let me do this before we have a medical emergency on our hands. Here, do something you are good at and open this bottle.' Lauren handed her sister the wine.

'Thanks! I am not completely hopeless!' Kate exclaimed.

'Now then you two!' Shirley tutted in mock exasperation.

'Seriously, Kate,' said Lauren, 'thank you for taking me along last night, I had a lovely time.'

'No problem! It really was a *great* night, wasn't it? And you were the belle of the ball, dancing with Erik like that. He was really interested in you.'

'Nonsense. He was just being polite. There were so many gorgeous women there, why would he be interested in me?' A small part of her wished that wasn't true. She had enjoyed herself, far more than she expected. It had been a real taste of glamour and excitement. It would have been lovely if it could have gone on forever. *Oh well, it was fun while it lasted.* 'What could a man like Erik Danielsen possibly see in someone as quiet and boring as me?'

'Ah! But if it's in the stars... it will be so! Guardian angels will make sure we all reach our fated destinies – besides, you're *not* boring.'

Lauren stared incredulously at her younger sister. 'What *on earth* are you talking about? You can't possibly believe that!'

'Yup. I've been studying astrology and the theory of reincarnation. I think we've all been here before in previous lives. We don't remember them of course, but we were always together and when we die our souls go to the stars or back up into the universe.' Kate faltered, looking slightly perplexed, then shrugged. 'Well, I don't know *exactly* where we go, but we are all stardust, aren't we? I saw that in a documentary on the Science channel.' She continued more confidently. 'So, then we have to wait...and our spirits get chosen again when the time is right and we get to live again. Together. To fulfil our own destinies! Until we don't need to learn anymore and we have achieved all we can. We become our 'ultimate selves' – but James doesn't believe me. He thinks it's all silly nonsense and says I read too much.'

'For once, I actually agree with him,' said Lauren. 'I am almost afraid to ask...' Lauren placed her wine glass in front of her with extra caution... 'But what happens then? When we have all become our 'ultimate selves'?'

'Well...' Kate's brow furrowed, a look of perplexed concentration on her face. 'I think maybe we get to be guardian angels. You know - helping others along the way.'

Lauren opened her mouth to exclaim in disbelief, but their mother beat her to it.

'Goodness, what an imagination you have!' she said. 'The

very idea that you will be helping any unfortunate person along their way through life! You'd have to pity that poor soul. Come and eat. If you're going to be a guardian angel, my girl, you will need all the strength you can muster. Gretchen, go to your basket, there's a good girl. Chester, leave the cat *alone!*'

Dinner passed pleasantly, then James called to take Kate to the cinema and after they'd gone Lauren began to help Shirley with the washing up.

'So, you enjoyed yourself last night?' asked Shirley. 'You had a nice time?'

'Yes, but Erik wouldn't be interested in seeing me again, Mum.'

Shirley sighed in exasperation. 'Lauren, you mustn't put yourself down, darling. You are attractive, intelligent and interesting.' She touched her arm lightly. 'Sometimes, the best girls have to be patient for the worthiest men to come along.'

'Thanks, Mum. It's just, well… I am a realist, I suppose. Erik leads a very different life to mine. His life is very cosmopolitan and glamorous. He's practically a celebrity in the business world we would be like chalk and cheese! I am sure he was being polite, that's all.'

'Well, Kate seems to think otherwise, darling, and she was there.'

'Kate *would* think so! She's always trying to make some drama out of nothing. You know what an over-active imagination she has.'

'Maybe so.' Shirley put down a plate she had been drying. 'But she is also astute, sharp-minded and she doesn't miss much. Besides, she loves you and wouldn't have encouraged you to go if she thought this Erik wasn't genuine.'

'Well, yes… though now he's had a chance to spend some

time with me, I will probably never see him again.' Lauren shrugged. 'So that's that. And it's OK.'

However, even as she spoke, some tiny part of her wasn't as certain of this as she sounded.

* * *

Upon returning home alone, Lauren felt a flat, despondent mood creep over her after the unexpected excitement of her birthday. She decided to distract herself by practising the piano, but it didn't help lift her mood. She must have played this part of a concerto by Tchaikovsky twenty times…was she *ever* going to master it? Maybe she'd ask her mother to help her later in the week. For now, she needed a break. Lauren got up from her piano with Gretchen at her heels and went to the kitchen, flicked the switch of the kettle and daydreamed out of the window. It was a pleasant evening, crimson and gold drawing right across the sky.

Maybe there would be a film on TV later. Or maybe there was something decent showing at the cinema?

As she poured hot water into her mug for coffee she heard the purr of an engine labour along her driveway and stop right outside her house. An unfamiliar grey Audi A6 Quattro stopped in her driveway. Through the window, Lauren saw a slim, elegant woman in her mid-thirties carrying a battered black leather medical bag approach the house.

When the knock at the door came, she crossed the hallway. Gretchen beat her to it, bad leg forgotten, tail thumping against the doorframe expectantly.

Lauren opened the door. 'May I help you?' Maybe the stranger was lost and had stopped to ask directions; it wouldn't be the first time this had happened.

'Hello, are you Lauren Sinclair?' The woman's voice had a musical lilt with a soft French accent.

How did this beauty know her name? She looked vaguely familiar, although for the life of her Lauren couldn't figure out why.

'Yes, I'm Lauren,' she said.

'I am Janelle DelaCroix.' The woman smiled prettily. 'My partner Greg Harrington treated your German Shepherd the other day. I was passing by and I thought perhaps I should call and check on her progress. I hope it's a convenient time?'

'Oh! Yes of course! Thank you for thinking of us. Please, do come in.'

So this was Greg's partner. She was truly stunning, with her clear, honey-coloured complexion, sapphire blue eyes and shiny long dark hair twisted loosely into a sophisticated chignon at the nape of her slender neck.

Janelle approached Gretchen confidently with a few friendly words and dropped easily to kneel beside her, all the while speaking to her in a calm, gentle manner. Lauren lowered herself on Gretchen's opposite side, ready to offer assistance if necessary. She was so close to Janelle she could pick up faint traces of her floral perfume. Rose and jasmine, warm and classy.

'Well, as you can see, she's fine now.' Lauren smiled. Gretchen thumped her tail in response and regarded this new visitor inquisitively, sniffing the edge of her coat in hope of a treat.

'Well, her leg certainly seems sound enough,' Janelle announced cheerfully, producing the expected biscuit from her coat pocket. 'Superb breed. I love the shepherds, they're so intelligent and eager to please. Where did you get her from?'

'She was my mother's idea. We found a great breeder in

Okehampton. All her puppies were simply gorgeous; I chose this little madam because she was so good-natured, and came running straight to me. She loves being the centre of attention!' Lauren laughed. 'Thank you so much. It's very good of you to call. I was desperately worried when she injured herself, but Josh was so helpful. He told me he wanted to study to be a vet at Exeter University. You must be so proud of him.'

'Yes, he's a good lad. We are lucky. He works hard and often helps us at the practice.'

'I was just making coffee – would you like some?'

'That's very kind of you, but I'm afraid I must be going.' Janelle looked apologetic.

Of course, Lauren reasoned. It was getting late and no doubt Greg was waiting for her.

'If you need anything else, please call us, any time.' She smiled warmly at Lauren and handed her a business card at the door.

'I will. Thank you.'

After she'd gone, Lauren put the business card on the hall table and made a mental note to call the practice about their puppy training classes. Gretchen was intelligent and quick to learn, she would certainly benefit from some socialisation.

Come to think of it, so would she.

5

Surprises

Through the window, Lauren could see Julia standing in front of Heaven Scent, a little ball of brownish grey fur wriggling in her arms. 'Sorry I'm late! Craig thought it might be good to get a puppy.' She smiled a little hesitantly. 'I've just been to the vet's to get his shots.'

'Oh, lovely! A playmate for Gretchen!' Lauren smiled. On closer inspection she was surprised. 'What made you choose a mastiff?'

'Craig's parents had one when he was growing up. This little fella came from the pound, they had a litter there last week and they desperately needed homes for them. Luckily, by the time we got there they had found homes for them all except this little chap – and he was running out of time. Well… we went to see him and we just couldn't leave him there to be put to sleep. Besides, Craig thought he'd be good company for me while he's at work.' Julia's voiced faltered a little. 'He is lovely natured. But perhaps a bit bigger than I thought he would be.'

'He's a mastiff!' Lauren laughed. 'He's going to get a lot bigger yet! Why not check out the puppy socialisation training classes at the vet's rooms in town next week? I'm going to take Gretchen along, I've heard they're very good. It's so important to get off to a good start and learn how to train your new puppy properly. Would you like to come with me? I could meet you there.'

* * *

On Wednesday evening Lauren and Gretchen headed towards the welcoming yellow glow of the Harrington Veterinary Surgery to meet Julia for an evening of puppy socialisation fun and training. They could hear laughter and excited yipping drifting through the air towards them as they got closer to the venue. Lauren pushed open the door and the noise reached a crescendo. Gretchen eyed the other young dogs and puppies happily, eager to join the fun, recent sore leg and limping now completely forgotten.

'Lauren! Over here! Hi!' came a cheerful cry from a flustered Elaine, lifting her West Highland puppy out of the small dogs' play pen. Matthew squealed and danced behind her in sheer delight.

Lauren lightly kissed her best friend on the cheek and tickled the wriggling white ball of fluff under the chin. 'Oh my! What have we got here?'

'A puppy, for the family!' Paul grinned and slipped his arm around his wife's shoulders. "Meet Maxwell!"

'Apparently, he'll be a good companion for our children.' Elaine rolled her eyes, but her smile gave away her good humour. 'So now I will *really* have my hands full.'

'Just in time! Class is just about to start. Please take your puppies and have a seat.' A prim middle-aged veterinary nurse in a crisp white coat indicated the chairs placed around the edge of the room.

Everyone settled and an expectant hush descended, all eyes on the nurse in-charge of the class. She stood and pointed to a whiteboard precariously propped on an easel in the middle of the room. 'Now, who can tell me...,' she began.

Suddenly, the door flew open with a bang, and a flustered Craig was pulled into the room by a large, slobbering, over-exuberant blur of grey fur, followed shyly by Julia.

'Hello everyone, sorry we're late,' Craig announced. 'We've been for a walk to try and calm him down a bit.' Buddy had clearly enjoyed every moment of his muddy walk and delighted in being the centre of attention among so many interesting prospective new friends.

'Kindly call him to heel now and take a seat,' the nurse admonished. 'Class has already begun.'

'OK, sure.' Craig attempted to rein in Buddy, who was straining at his leash, eyeing each of the puppies in turn and eagerly wanting to play. He clearly had no intention of sitting down and listening any time soon, there was far too much to investigate.

'We'll just sit over here then. Come on boy,' Craig coaxed.

'Will you please take a seat!' the nurse commanded, folding her arms across her ample bosom.

'Yes, I'm sorry He's just a bit excited – Buddy! NOOO!'

Buddy had slipped out of his collar and, gleeful with newfound freedom, bounded across the classroom. He spied a pretty little Labrador in a corner, who looked as if she might like a game of chase, and made a beeline for her.

The little Labrador girl emitted a yip of surprise and took

off around the classroom in alarm, with Buddy hot on her heels.

Horrified, Craig jumped into action and threw his arms wide in an attempt to block Buddy's path and catch him, but a determined Buddy swerved and successfully evaded him.

The nurse looked on, aghast at the developing commotion. The Labrador puppy bolted towards her, with Buddy and Craig in hot pursuit.

Bravely, the nurse stood in front of her easel as if to protect it from the inevitable onslaught.

'Stop!' she ordered, hand raised in defiant command. 'Stop this instant!'

'STOP!'

Buddy had yet to learn the meaning of the command and distracted from his earlier goal, turned and headed straight for the nurse. Julia screamed and Craig closed his eyes. In a split second, Buddy completely destroyed the classroom, covering the nurse with muddy paw prints and sending the whiteboard flying against the wall, where it smashed into fragments.

The deafening crash sent Buddy hurtling back to Craig. The bedraggled nurse staggered and struggled to regain her composure. She looked slightly dazed as she tried to brush paw prints off her once pristine uniform and smoothed her ruffled hair into place.

'Crate!' she stammered, shakily pointing to a large black steel contraption in the corner.

Julia and Craig looked at each other in shame. This was too awful. It was the ultimate punishment. Poor Buddy was being sent to doggy school detention.

'CRATE!' the dishevelled nurse thundered, her face dark with rage. 'PUT. HIM. IN. THE. CRATE!'

* * *

The next afternoon there was a break in the weather as the snow turned to glistening droplets and melted, leaving the town shining. Lauren headed towards her shop. Blissful warmth enveloped her as she opened the door.

'Hi!' Julia smiled from behind the counter amid a beautifully opulent display of lilac, pink and white.

'On Monday we have three new orders. The customers want to collect from the shop. I asked them to be in by lunch time, is that OK?'

'Sure, thanks for that,' Lauren replied, wondering why the date seemed vaguely familiar. She had a feeling something was special about it, but couldn't remember why.

During the early afternoon Lauren made a start on making up the next day's orders. Julia was minding the shop front and Lauren felt quite content working in the back room. Glancing at the appointments book she realised why Monday was so noteworthy – it was Janelle's birthday, the day Greg had requested a large bouquet be made and delivered. Unfortunately, it was also the day their delivery van had been booked into the garage for a service and some minor repairs, which meant Craig had been given the day off.

She would have to attend to this delivery herself.

As she settled contentedly into the afternoon's work, her phone buzzed with a text message. Elaine was asking if she were free later and, if so, did she want to come to dinner tonight?

'Yes, please,' Lauren replied and smiled happily. She always loved spending time with Elaine and her family.

* * *

Two half-melted snow figures stood lopsidedly on the lawn of Elaine and Paul's front garden. A snowman and a snow dog presumably, although the smaller figure looked more like a snow armadillo, Lauren mused. The door was flung open and Lauren found herself stepping over an array of different sized wellington boots and colourful toys that littered the entrance.

'Come in, come in!' Paul boomed cheerfully, swinging the door open wide to let Lauren and Gretchen in. Matthew giggled, clearly loving seeing the world from his new, higher perspective on his father's shoulders. Maxwell yipped and jumped excitedly at his feet.

'Hi, hon!' Elaine called in greeting from the kitchen.

Lauren handed her a colourful posy. 'Hi! Thanks for inviting me. It's so good to see you!'

'Hope you're hungry. I've been baking today and I want you to try these. It's a new recipe.' Elaine produced a plate of chocolate brownies.

'They look amazing!' Lauren rarely cooked and almost never baked. She took half a brownie and nibbled on it; it was smooth, rich and really very good indeed.

Elaine lifted a dish of bubbling lasagne from the oven, placed it on the counter and turned to open her fridge. It was jam-packed full of dishes; casseroles and roast meats, stewed and fresh fruits, mixed vegetables, a large colourful trifle and an array of drinks. How did she manage it? Lauren wondered. Her own fridge was quite empty in comparison - although, of course, she didn't have a family to care for. The most used appliance in her house was the kettle. Her fridge contained three bottles of wine, some chocolates, champagne, milk – and very little else.

'Can I give you a hand?' Lauren asked

'Nope, it's all done. Drink?'

'Whatever you are having.'

'I'm not drinking at the moment. It's lemonade.' Elaine gestured to her glass.

'Yup, that's fine. Wait – is there something you need to tell me?'

Elaine's eyes danced with happiness. 'Yes, I'm expecting again.'

'Oh, hon, that's wonderful!' Lauren reached to hug her friend. 'Congratulations! How far along are you?'

'About twelve weeks. I'm not sure I'd describe the morning sickness as 'wonderful' but thanks. We only just told our folks this week.'

'I am pleased for you. I know you've been wanting another baby for some time.' Lauren was genuinely pleased for Elaine, but felt a twinge of regret. Would she ever have a family of her own? She pushed aside the wave of hurt and swallowed an unexpected lump in her throat. This wasn't about her. It was great news for Elaine...

After a glorious dinner, the washing up was done and the fire lit. Gradually the pace of the evening's activities slowed. Dusk turned into night. An aura of comfortable contentment settled over the family like a soft blanket. Lauren felt a pang of desire as she watched Matthew kiss his mother goodnight and toddle sleepily into his father's arms to be carried upstairs to bed. How lucky Elaine was to be happily married with a young family she thought, not for the first time. But she mustn't be jealous. Elaine was her best friend and she loved her; she deserved all she had.

'Did Paul mention we are having his niece stay with us for a while?'

Lauren, who had been mesmerised by the flickering gold of the fire, turned her attention to her friend. 'No… I don't think so.'

'Paul's older sister is migrating to Australia with her new husband. They have to buy a house and settle into new jobs, so we said we would take in Rebecca for a few months. She's seventeen.

'I'm hoping she might see it as a break from study and a country holiday, and also give me a hand around the place!' Elaine's eyes twinkled. 'Although I expect at that age she will want to do her own thing. I just hope she isn't too bored here.'

'Hmm. I hope she isn't a handful for you.' Lauren remembered all too well what her sister had been like at that age.

Elaine chuckled. 'Well, she'll have to do as she's told. I think she is basically a good girl. She loves reading and horses, apparently rides very well. She worked hard at school and did well last year so her mum thought she deserved a treat and holiday would do her good. Come to us one evening next week and meet her, if you like. We'll have a supper and games evening. It'll be good fun.'

'Sounds good! I might just do that,' Lauren agreed.

After bidding her friends farewell she stepped into the cold with mixed feelings. It had been great to catch up, but a feeling of regret, like a deep uncertainty gnawing away at her insides, left her feeling cold. If only things had been different, this could have been her life.

* * *

As she approached her house, Lauren noticed the gate to her driveway was open. She was certain she had closed it behind her car as she always did. At the doorway she was surprised to find a large colourful bouquet filling the entrance.

Mystified, she carefully carried it through to the kitchen. Lauren couldn't remember the last time anyone had bought her flowers. And these were truly magnificent: glorious Calla lilies and perfect little tea roses frothing all over the kitchen table in her favourite colours. Nestled at the centre was a single, perfect, deep red rose with a small golden envelope attached to the stem. Her name was written in a distinguished neat scroll on the front. She didn't recognise the writing. Whoever were these from?

The gold-edged card had the watermarked emblem of an exclusive designer florist in the city. Two theatre tickets fell onto the table as Lauren opened the card: *Thank you for a perfect evening. Hope you will accept these as a belated birthday gift. Looking forward to seeing you again – Erik.*

Lauren felt a surge of elation, which was quickly replaced by a wave of anxiety. Good heavens! The last thing she had expected was to be asked out by Erik Danielsen again. A thousand panicky questions flooded her mind.

Calm down!

She studied the tickets. Saturday night. She was free that night so she would be able to go. If she wanted to. What was she thinking? Of course she did! But….how *could* she go? Her heart hammered against her breastbone at the thought of a proper date with the handsome business celebrity. Exciting! She sank onto the sofa, dizzy with anxiety and amazement.

How will I ever sleep tonight?

* * *

'I just stopped by to see how you are and wanted to tell

you… Ooh! Who are these from?' Kate walked straight over to the flowers. 'Oh.My.God. They are to *die* for! Tell me, tell me, tell me, tell me…'

Lauren threw an exasperated look at her sister. Couldn't she see she was talking on the phone?

'OK.' Lauren lowered the phone. 'Be quiet for two seconds so I can get a word in edgeways and I will *be able* to tell you. Perhaps. If you promise not to tell everyone else you know.'

'Ooh! A mystery admirer! Now you have got to tell me,' Kate squealed in excitement.

'No big mystery. If you must know, it was Erik who sent them, a belated birthday gift and, well…to ask me out on a date this weekend. I was just talking to him when you interrupted.' Lauren tried to sound nonchalant.

Kate stared at her.

'Ah! Silence is golden!' Lauren laughed. She'd rarely seen her younger sister lost for words.

'Erik sent them? See? I told you he liked you, I was sure of it.'

'Hmmm. So it would seem. He's quite the perfect gentleman.' Lauren smiled. 'I must admit, I didn't see it coming. Took me by surprise, I can tell you.'

'Coffee?' Lauren flicked the kettle on.

'Go on, then. I'm exhausted. I could certainly use it.' Kate sank gratefully onto a kitchen chair and absent-mindedly scratched Gretchen behind the ear.

'So, what did you want to tell me?'

'Oh yes! I've got some news!' Kate grinned. 'You know I've been working so much overtime? Well, it's finally paid off. I've been given my own portfolio.' She beamed proudly.

'Kate, that's wonderful! 'I'm so pleased for you. Well

done! Tell me all about it – who's it for?'

'Mulberry Park. They manufacture childcare products and I have to sort out their entire insurance package. It's actually one of the biggest orders we've ever had.'

'Well, it sounds very interesting. Quite a responsibility, I imagine?'

'It is! It's the biggest portfolio I've worked on and I want it to be superb. Cynthia Martell went for it too. You know, the new girl. She told me she had been given similar portfolios at her last job, so she's had prior experience. I wasn't at all sure I'd be picked for it, but I got it. I know I can do this. I've been *sooo* looking forward to a chance like this!'

'That's fantastic, Katie.'

'I know! James says he's so proud of me. We're going out to a club to celebrate with some of his friends, although I would have preferred a meal or perhaps just a quiet drink.' Kate looked a little rueful. 'I have so much homework to do. I have to study my client's requirements and I really would have liked to get a head start tonight, but James says I must take the chance to meet his friends and celebrate; this is my chance to shine. Lauren, this is *huge*. I can't wait!'

Lauren tried not to wince at the mention of James, and smiled at her sister's enthusiastic chatter. This would be a great opportunity for her. She had mentioned Cynthia before, and Lauren recalled the quiet, studious mousey-haired girl with the glasses who had watched her dance with Erik that night in Chansons.

In the quiet of the evening, after Kate had left to meet James, Lauren reflected on her earlier conversation with Erik. He had called her to ask if she had liked the flowers and confirm their date. She had recognised his voice with its soft northern accent at once, so calm and self-assured. Surprisingly gentle for a man with so much responsibility. She had thanked him for the flowers and accepted his invitation graciously. In truth she had wanted to ask him why he had chosen to ask her when he spent a good deal of his busy life surrounded by far prettier girls. Now that was a real mystery. But of course she hadn't; that would have made her sound insecure.

And it didn't matter anyway, because he had asked *her,* Lauren thought happily.

* * *

Kate arrived at James's chosen venue and made her way to the bar.

'Here she is!' She turned at the sound of his voice booming over the top of the chatter and music. 'My shining star!'

He smiled and Kate felt herself grow three inches taller. She adored James and felt so lucky to have such a successful and popular boyfriend. If only they could do more things by themselves occasionally. Perhaps have some quiet evenings together. But James was a socialite and insisted the importance of networking and social connection should never be underestimated. He believed you had to 'be out there' to stay successful. Promote yourself. Never miss an opportunity to highlight every success. At once, Kate felt guilty. He was thinking of her, celebrating her promotion. She shouldn't be so ungrateful. She pushed thoughts of tiredness and guilt about homework away and allowed herself to be led to the bar and become encircled by a group of influential strangers.

6

Fortuity

Lauren drove steadily over the moors to the Harrington residence to deliver a large, gorgeously frothing mixed bouquet of pink and white. She had personally made up the order, wanting to make sure it was perfect as a way of repaying Greg and Janelle for their care of Gretchen, and was proud of her creation. It included chrysanthemums in various coral tones, flamingo and sugar pink Casa Blanca lilies, delicate mauve orchids, blush narcissus, two-toned candy and baby pink Queen Ann's lace, bright fuchsia Star of Bethlehem and exquisite little tea roses in vibrant shades of raspberry, cerise and carmine that were so perfect they looked as if they were made of porcelain. All this was topped off with layer upon layer of pure white frothing gypsophila. The bouquet had taken hours to perfect and the result was simply stunning.

Following the automated voice directions on her GPS, she found herself deep in an expansive canvas of beautiful English moorland countryside. As she neared her destination an impressive Georgian building came into view. The double black wrought iron gates were open and she turned into the drive and slowly made her way towards the imposing building, with its immaculate formal gardens.

Lauren felt slightly nervous; the last time she had seen Greg the conversation had been stilted and awkward. She would have preferred Craig to deliver the bouquet. Still, someone had to do it and she was here now.

My word, this place was really something. It was as if she'd stepped out of her car straight into an oil painting. The air seemed fresher up here and she spent a moment taking in the sweetness.

A tranquil stillness and the scent of fresh pine faintly tinged with wood-smoke from the chimneys relaxed her and cleared her mind, freeing her thoughts and imagination. She carefully lifted the weighty bouquet from the back seat of her car and walked towards the house, bathed in the pale radiance of late afternoon light. Any tension and uncertainty vanished and a reassuring calm surrounded her.

Lauren felt at once intrigued and comfortable. The gardens extended a sense of welcome and the house seemed to emanate protectiveness. Strangely, it was as if she had been here long ago and was returning home.

There was no answer at the front door and she felt uneasy about leaving the bouquet on the doorstep; the delicate blooms would need fresh water and shelter from the winter chill. She pushed apprehension aside and ventured around the side of the property with the flowers. Perhaps there would be someone there she could leave them with.

No one seemed to be around, however, and the only detectable sounds were the bird songs in the trees. Towards the rear of the house Lauren stopped and sat on a wooden bench for a few minutes to enjoy the view. Ancient hills divided into a patchwork quilt of fields in emerald, mustard, russet and gold, rolled ever onward into the distance. Miniature trees and buildings dotted the tranquil scene, the tiny white sheep reminding her of a toy farm. Before her, Lauren spotted familiar landmarks, farms and villages she had come to know and love.

The crisp country air relaxed and soothed her soul and for a few minutes, she allowed herself to be transported back in time, to her younger years spent hiking and exploring the countryside with her grandparents during school holidays. Lauren closed her eyes to enjoy the tranquillity. After a time, she heard the faint sound of horses' hooves in the distance that gradually grew louder, followed by mumbled voices cutting into the peace that had surrounded her. She listened for a few minutes, then decided to investigate in the hope of finding someone to accept the delivery. She followed the voices into a wooded area adjacent to the house. After a few hundred metres she found herself opposite a stable, where a lean black cat stared at her with wide yellow eyes, then magically disappeared into the building over a wooden door.

Hefty hooves clipped along the stone path and male voices gradually became clearer.

Greg rounded the corner of the yard, spattered with mud and leading a large, fine-looking dark chestnut stallion. He was talking to a lean, grey haired man, his skin tanned and creased by the weather in his sixties, maybe even seventies. Lauren couldn't tell. She was spellbound, suddenly and unexpectedly breathless.

He was even more handsome than she remembered, with streaks of silver highlighting his dark, unruly hair and his skin smooth and evenly tanned. He looked relaxed and in control, commanding the great horse with ease.

Greg stopped abruptly when he saw her, a look of surprise giving way to a slight frown. He dismounted without taking his gaze from her.

'Well, hello again. I didn't expect you to deliver Janelle's flowers in person.'

Lauren caught her breath. Dammit, he was gorgeous. No wonder he was taken. Heat flooded her cheeks at the thought and she gave herself an inward shake.

'Hello there!' She managed a smile. 'My delivery driver was unavailable so I brought them myself but no one answered the door.'

'Well, thank you for coming all the way out here.'

'Not at all, it's my pleasure.'

She walked over to the horse and stroked his velvety smooth nose, feeling the steady rhythm of his warm breath on her hand.

'He's superb!' she murmured. 'Is he yours?'

'Yes, I have three. All thoroughbreds. I bred this boy myself. Aaron can be a real character at times.' Greg patted the stallion's muscular neck and handed the reins to his older companion. 'Tom, would you take him, please?'

'Aaron' Lauren mused as the horse was led away. 'Means strength doesn't it?'

'Apparently so. 'Mountains of strength', so Josh tells me. He chose the name, and it's a very good name for this boy, he's never let me down. Do you ride?'

'Yes, or rather, I used to. Kate – that's my sister – and I loved riding as children. Our grandparents had two gentle old Welsh ponies, Toby and Bess. I would ride them all summer long if my parents let me!'

Greg smiled. 'A kindred spirit then.' He indicated to the bouquet. Why don't we take those into the kitchen and I'll show you around – that is, if you have time?'

'I'd love to, thank you.'

* * *

Lauren thoroughly enjoyed her tour around the grounds and stables. The awkwardness of their previous meeting was quickly dissolved by their shared love of horses and riding. Greg introduced her to a beautiful chestnut mare and her mate, Aaron's sire. All three were large, muscular thoroughbreds and their coats shone with beautiful condition. The mare had a gentle manner about her. 'They are stunning, Greg.' Lauren stroked the mare's velvety nose.

Greg chuckled. 'That's Maya. She's the oldest, and mother of Aaron. He was intended for Josh before he moved out. This is his father, Kane. He's my boy but can be a bit of a handful when the mood takes him.'

'I'll bet he can!' The powerful stallion seemed to fill all the available space in his stall, standing proudly as if he knew he was special.

They left the stables then and strolled companionably through the garden together, the mellow sunlight bathing their surroundings in a golden glow as it began to fade. Greg indicated to a wooden bench roughly cut from a felled tree, and Lauren sat. The bench was surprisingly comfortable with a deep seat and high back. Greg's thigh brushed hers as he joined her, setting butterflies fluttering in her stomach at his touch.

'Are you cold?' He looked concerned.

She shook her head and smiled. She could hardly feel cold sitting so close to him.

Sunbeams fell across the garden and alighted upon an ancient silver birch tree, naked of leaves, its gnarled branches weaving an intricate web-like silhouette against the darkening sky. The silver trunk standing nobly straight and tall despite its great age glowed slightly in the afternoon light, like the spirit of an old soldier, Lauren mused.

'Beautiful,' she murmured breathlessly, studying the tree's changing image, that seemed to breathe with new life each time the light changed; first, a light golden yellow hue which slowly darkened to blood orange; then patches of soft crimson and pink developed and spread, breaking out over the entire body of the tree.

'Yes.'

Greg's voice was low, his lips close to her ear. She felt her heart skip a beat, and everything around her seemed to fall into the distance, further and further away.

'It was planted by my great-grandfather. Josh called it 'the magical rainbow tree' when he was little.' There was a smile in his voice as he stretched out his arms and legs, casually letting an arm fall behind her across the back of the seat. Lauren wanted more than anything to ease into his arm and snuggle into his side. Her resolve kept her upright and still, aware they both had other commitments and not wanting to change the newly found blissful contentment between them.

'You should see it in the summer; it's magnificent covered in foliage. But I think it's even more special at this time of year.'

She nodded, 'Yes. It's simply breathtaking. Amazing – I have never seen anything quite like it, the way the colours alight and dance on the bark. It seems to make it fade into the background then somehow come alive and glow again – almost an illusion.'

'Quite like a mirage!' he exclaimed.

'The illusion of the mirage tree,' Lauren murmured, radiant with delight at sharing a special moment with this wonderful man. Almost as if he read her mind, Greg nodded in agreement, sharing her enthusiasm. 'That's exactly what I was thinking!'

Walking slowly back to the house Lauren wanted to savour every moment of their enchanting afternoon together. She lingered at row of pure white winter rose bushes. The delicate petals of the large blooms were flawless and almost translucent.

'Oh, these are just gorgeous!' she said. This garden seemed full of enchantments. 'My word! Who's the gardener?'

Greg chuckled. 'All thanks to Tom. My father planted them many years ago. Actually, we all love gardening, but find we don't have much time these days.'

Lauren tumbled back to reality, the chemistry between them dispelled at thoughts of Janelle.

He stooped to pick a Helleborus rose and carefully handed it to her. She accepted it gracefully; intensely aware of the few brief seconds his fingers brushed hers in an almost intimate gesture.

'Would you like to come to dinner tonight? You'd be very welcome,' he asked.

'Well, thank you, um…it's very kind of you to ask but, well, I couldn't...' she stammered in confusion, caught off guard. The idea of spending more time in his company was definitely appealing. But back to reality. Enough whimsical fantasizing.

'I couldn't possibly impose on such a special occasion,' she said, pushing down the stab of regret. 'Greg, it's been lovely, but I had better get going, and leave you to do what you have to. Thank you so much for a wonderful afternoon!'

'Of course. No problem at all, it's been my pleasure. Another time perhaps.'

Did he look a little disappointed? Surely not – her imagination was playing tricks again. Best she left now, let him get on with his business.

Besides, she had to prepare for her date at the theatre with the amazing Erik Danielsen. The fleeting thought that perhaps it was the wrong person taking her to the theatre crossed her mind. She pulled herself up sharply. Erik was awesome and she was determined to enjoy the evening. Greg belonged to Janelle. That's just how it was.

* * *

Much later that evening, Lauren folded her hands into her lap in an attempt to stop any nervous fidgeting. Sinking into the soft leather interior of the smart new BMW Erik had sent for her she glanced out of the window. Orange and white street and window lights blurred into one as the car smoothly passed them on the way to the theatre.

She tried to tell herself to relax and to enjoy the moment, but she felt butterflies in the pit of her stomach. Rarely had she been treated to such a smart evening out.

It had taken her an age to get ready and decide what to wear. In the end she had ignored her sister's advice to wear a sassy, brightly coloured cocktail dress and opted instead for a classically simple designer evening dress, black heels and a silver clutch purse. This was a whole new experience for her. And with Erik Danielsen! She would never have believed it possible.

The car pulled up at the side of the busy road outside the theatre and she spotted Erik waiting for her among the many people entering the foyer, looking elegantly handsome as ever. Taking a deep breath, she slipped out of the car as the door was held open for her and tried her best to walk confidently towards him. She saw him glance at his watch, then look around expectantly, a dazzling broad smile developing as he caught sight of her walking towards him through the crowd. Before she knew it, Erik was right beside her.

'Lauren! How wonderful to see you again. I am sorry I couldn't collect you personally, I had a late meeting with clients,' he explained. Leaning towards her he whispered, 'You look beautiful.'

She felt the warmth of his breath against her cheek as he kissed her lightly in greeting. 'Thank you,' she managed slightly breathlessly and stepped through the theatre door Erik held open for her with one arm, while the other shielded her shoulders protectively.

Their tickets had secured a private viewing box in the upper gallery. He took her hand, and as they made their way up the opulent staircase, carefully holding their champagne flutes, Lauren caught sight of a familiar face in the crowd. *Could it be Janelle? It was!* She looked stunning in a midnight blue silk designer dress that only a woman with such an exquisite figure could carry off. She smiled in greeting. Just behind her Greg held Lauren's gaze steadily and coolly inclined his head towards her. The words 'lucky lady' leapt into her mind. Quickly pushing them aside, she turned her concentration back to Erik and the evening ahead.

The performance was spellbinding. Lauren was transported to another time and place, immersed in the beautiful arias, and cocooned in the dark velvety warmth of the theatre. Every now and then she remembered she was with Erik. At one point during the last act he lightly took her hand and she smiled, aware he was watching her.

Stepping into the cool night air was a sharp reminder of the reality that it was winter. Lauren shivered slightly and pulled her shrug tightly around her shoulders.

'You're cold!' Erik exclaimed in concern. 'We can't have that! Come, let's find a nice warm bar to have a drink.'

He slipped his arm around her shoulders and led her across the street to a fashionable brightly lit wine bar buzzing with activity and excitement. A white light flashed as they entered the lounge area; Lauren looked up in surprise as she realised someone had taken their photograph. A few people had turned in their direction, whispering and looking curious.

Erik smiled reassuringly. 'Don't worry. It'll just be the local press, writing for their entertainment column.'

Lauren felt a bit disconcerted but pushed the feeling to the back of her mind and concentrated on the conversation. Champagne and canapés arrived at their table and Erik tried to make her feel as comfortable as possible. He wanted to know all about her; her interests, musical tastes and preferences. He complimented her on opening her own business. Lauren was pleased to find they had some common ground. Both enjoyed classical music, fine wine and dining, reading, films and theatre although when the conversation turned to hobbies, Erik's love of adventurous travel and strenuous winter sports left Lauren feeling out of her depth.

'To be honest, I prefer a quieter life. I don't travel much – I can't really, with my business, you see. I have to be there to run the shop and oversee the orders, and of course, there's

Gretchen.'

'Gretchen?' Erik looked puzzled. 'You have a daughter? Kate didn't mention her.'

Lauren laughed. 'Well she *is* my dependent, I suppose! But no, not my daughter. She's my companion, my German Shepherd dog.'

Erik smiled, bemused. 'I've never bothered much with animals. They are all right, I suppose, but I need to travel at a moment's notice for work. I need to be free to do whatever I want.'

'Yes, they can be a tie. But Gretchen has a beautiful temperament and is a great friend. I'm glad I found her.'

The conversation turned to current affairs, local news and entertainment and future plans. Lauren felt a little overwhelmed. Erik spoke of business trips planned in London and Paris and vacations in Northern Europe and America with friends and family. It all seemed remarkable and exciting to her, an entirely different world from her own.

In the car on the way home Lauren couldn't help smiling to herself. Despite the differences in their lifestyles, the evening had been a success, and she had enjoyed talking to him. They agreed to meet again the following weekend at a Valentine's Day piano recital in the city's music hall. Erik had suggested dinner afterwards and Lauren had readily agreed, delighted but slightly mystified. He must have many more glamorous dates who lived closer to his luxury apartment in the city. She wasn't at all sure she would enjoy city life. But none the less, she felt happy at the prospect of seeing him again.

* * *

Early the next morning Lauren happily flicked through

the shop's order book. With Valentine's Day just around the corner, business was picking up. She would have to make sure she had enough red roses. There were already six orders for large bouquets of red roses. She absentmindedly turned the page and a paragraph of Julia's neat handwriting caught her attention. A new order had come in. Glancing over it, Lauren sharply caught her breath.

Oh my goodness.

Could that possibly be right? *Forty-eight* red roses!

Whoever would possibly have ordered that many? Most gentlemen would consider six, or maybe a dozen roses for Valentines day, at a push. All the pretty single red roses in the gift boxes she and Julia had made up especially for the day would all sell, she was sure of it. But forty-eight roses! Lauren briefly considered calling Julia to check the order, but it was clearly written, as plain as day. One thing was certain; a bouquet this opulent was certainly going to impress one lucky lady.

Lauren double-checked the order. Yes, forty-eight red roses, for the morning of February fourteenth, to be delivered to –

Alverston Manor.

So, the lucky lady in question was Janelle. Greg must think the world of her. She made a mental note to get to the market early next week to collect the best stems before the Valentine's Day rush. She'd have to be there at daybreak.

The following evening Lauren and Gretchen ventured out to Elaine and Paul's house for their planned games evening. Carefully placed on the back seat of her car lay a pretty sunshine coloured posy of lilies and gerbera daisies and a bottle of Chardonnay.

They arrived just before six and Lauren juggled the wine and flowers as she knocked cheerfully on the door. It was swung open by a pretty young lady with long straight brown hair and an attractively freckled nose. She smiled shyly at Lauren as she stepped aside to let her in.

'Hello!' Lauren returned her smile warmly, 'You must be Rebecca. I'm Lauren. Pleased to meet you.'

'Hello' she responded. 'Call me Reba. We're all in here.' She gestured to the living room, vibrant with warm yellow light and the laughter of a game already in progress.

Lauren followed Reba through the doorway with Gretchen at her heels. She took one look at the scene in front of her in astonishment, and burst into laughter – her best friend was on the floor, leaning backwards on a gigantic colourful board on the floor, balanced on one hand and laughing. Matthew was sitting on the floor chuckling next to Paul, who watched his wife with concern. Josh was balanced on one leg and trying not to topple over.

Paul looked up and grinned at Lauren. 'Hi! Come on in. We're playing Twister. Elaine! Mind you don't fall!'

'Stop fussing!' she laughed as he held her arm and helped her up. 'I'll go get us some snacks.'

In the kitchen the two friends chatted while Lauren arranged the flowers in a blue china vase and Elaine collected various items from the fridge, cupboards and drawers, slicing, chopping and boiling water for tea in her matter-of-fact manner.

'Reba knows Josh from college and I'm so pleased she has a friend her own age here already. He seems so nice. They both like the same things too, which is lovely. They're talking about going for a few hikes on the moor when the weather cheers up a bit.'

'Great! Something for them to look forward too.' Lauren picked up a heavily laden tray and helped Elaine carry the tea things to the dining room.

During the evening, Lauren got a chance to chat with Josh.

'How's Gretchen doing?' he asked.

'Good now, thanks to you and your father. I was – still am – so grateful to you both.'

'That's OK. It was nothing. I was glad to help and I knew either Dad or Janelle would be able to fix her up.' He glanced at Gretchen who was happily aware she was the focus of attention and pleased to be seeing her friend again. Josh tickled her behind her ear.

'Well, madam is perfectly fine now. It's great you have a friend in town.' She smiled at Reba who came and sat next to Josh on the couch to join their conversation. 'How long have you two been friends?'

'Since the end of college last term. I've been so looking forward to coming here. I knew Josh lived nearby and we both love walking and camping. I can't wait for the weather to get a bit better so we can go explore the moors.'

'It will be great!' he enthused. 'I know a place near the ancient drovers' track where there are amazing panoramic views. Some of the best Dartmoor has to offer - and they recently discovered an ancient stone row, dating to 3500 BC. Nine granite stones oriented in a northeast to southwest direction, just like a mini Stonehenge. Amazing!'

'Wow! Well, that's certainly something to see.' Lauren recalled she had read something in the local paper about an important ancient stone monument being found recently on Dartmoor. This must be what Josh meant.

'It's an amazing discovery,' said Reba. 'A very significant prehistoric find. I can't wait to go exploring!'

A little later, Lauren followed Elaine into the kitchen to help prepare supper.

'How are you going with Erik what's-his-name?' Elaine asked. 'Is he nice? He treats you well?'

'Yes, very well. He's polite, charming and interesting. I'm not sure how well suited we are to be honest… but he truly is very nice.'

'Do you know anything about the Valentine's Ball in town next week?'

'Nothing really, except that I have a ton of new orders at the shop to work through. I don't think I'll make it. Erik mentioned going to a piano recital in the city so I'm quite looking forward to that.'

'Lovely!' Elaine approved. 'That sounds perfect.'

'Yes, maybe.'

'Well, as long as he's making you happy, just relax, go with the flow and enjoy it. See how it goes. That's all you can do. Just take one day at a time.'

Lauren knew it was good advice. She heard all this before, from her mother, Kate and now Elaine, she realised. Perhaps they were all right. Perhaps she really needed to stop worrying, dismiss doubts about the future and whether or not she and Erik were a good match and try to enjoy herself.

Silently, Lauren vowed to try. From now on, she would try to be more open to new possibilities.

7

'You're a superstar!' Kate sang as she walked into the kitchen and dropped a newspaper onto the table.

Lauren looked up from the accounts she was going through. 'What in heaven's name are you talking about?'

'You're only *famous!* Kate giggled and gestured to the paper. Mum gave this to me. Everyone in the village will have seen it by now.'

Lauren caught her breath at the brunette with the enigmatic expression looking directly back at her from the front page of the paper, Erik smiling confidently beside her.

'Oh my!' she exclaimed.

'Beautiful photo of you two,' Kate remarked. 'Really captured your good side. You look lovely, I just wished you'd smiled a bit more…'

'Oh, Kate, shut up! I had no idea it was being taken.'

'Ha! Well, I think it's great. By the way, Mum asked if we wanted to have lunch with her this Saturday when she gets back from walking with her friends. She says we should have a catch-up.'

'Yes, that's a good idea. I'll look forward to it. Julia can mind the shop for a couple of hours.' Lauren studied the photo again and shook her head. 'Goodness, me on the front page of the paper.'

'Well, if you are going to date the wealthiest, most successful and most handsome man in the South West of England, get used to it!' Kate laughed.

* * *

Elaine didn't window shop often. Her life always seemed too busy, her mornings spent caring for little Matthew, cooking and cleaning and afternoons going through the accounts and appointments for Paul's business. A shopping trip in Plymouth with Reba was a rare treat.

Paul had bought surprise tickets for the Tavistock Lions Club Valentine's Day Charity Ball next week and, as pregnancy didn't allow for much alteration of her existing wardrobe, he had agreed Elaine should buy herself a new dress. Reba would be going with Josh and also needed a suitable outfit, so after leaving Matthew with his grandmother, the two of them had set off to enjoy an afternoon together. Elaine was thoroughly enjoying her freedom from the usual household chores and loved discovering Reba's youthful fresh attitude to life.

They had just exited the shopping mall to head to a small café when she noticed a smart silver car glide smoothly into view and stop opposite the offices where Kate worked. It was difficult *not* to notice. A silver Maserati GranCabrio.

Very swish! How the other half lived!

As she took her seat near the window in the café, grateful to take the weight off her feet, she glanced again at the car.

The passenger door opened and she froze. A cold chill of recognition shot through her.

The driver was that gorgeous guy Erik what's-his-name Lauren was dating. She'd seen the papers. She'd recognise him anywhere. Blond, tanned, breathtaking smile…but who was this amazing supermodel-like creature with him? Elegantly clad from head to toe, she was flirting with him familiarly, kissing him warmly on both cheeks, holding his hand, smiling and suggestively squeezing his thigh.

The glamazon held his gaze as she swung her tanned, toned legs out of the car. Standing tall in spiked three inch Jimmy Choos, her dark hair swung over her face, obscuring Elaine's view of her features as she leaned in to speak to him as if she couldn't bear to be parted from him.

Then it was over – both vanished in a heartbeat; him in a metallic flash of shining silver and she a blur of grey Armani, darting into an office block. As Elaine stared at the space where they had been it felt surreal, as if they had never actually been there.

For a moment Elaine considered following the woman to find out who she was; but that was a ridiculous idea and besides, who would she ask for once inside the office block? Thoughtfully, she turned away from the window.

She would have to tell Lauren. It wouldn't be right not to.

* * *

Clara stormed through the office like a whirlwind, her mood as black as ink. She slammed the door shut without uttering a word to anyone. Her colleagues fell silent and kept their heads down. They knew better than to approach her when she was in this frame of mind. Sitting at the desk with her door firmly closed and the shutters drawn, Clara kicked off her stilettos and ran her fingers through her hair.

The lunch meeting had gone well, she and Erik were a first class team. She knew that. They complemented one another perfectly. He was the tough, authoritative leader and she played her part as attractive and supportive partner. She was smart though – and he knew it. She had a razor-like intuition, as flawless as any diamond. She watched his every move, read his every thought, anticipated every detail and backed him up at every turn. Together they *never* failed to charm even the toughest clients, *never* lost a contract, *always* won their mark. The two of them made a simply unbeatable team.

So why did he keep knocking her back?

Frustration gnawed away at her, tearing at her insides. She had done everything she could possibly think of to encourage him. He wasn't gay – she was absolutely sure of that. So why? When she had done everything she could to encourage him?

Everything.

She was sick and tired of making it crystal clear. Why couldn't he see they would make the perfect couple? What did she have to do to make him see how devoted to him she was? Every time she mentioned a celebratory drink for the two of them, or asked that snooty assistant of his to arrange a special date, or hinted at a well-deserved luxury weekend away for two, he would smile and brush her off with some jovial excuse, always polite but cool and out of reach.

It was strictly business with Erik.

Always business.

Clara took her head in her hands and massaged her aching temples. She blamed that bloody birthday girl, Lauren what's-her-name. All curves, shiny brown hair and smiles. Squeaky clean, the homely type who belonged in a soap advert. Anger flooded through her. Erik seemed completely besotted with her, although only God knew why. She looked as if she'd be more at home baking apple pies than showing Erik a good time in the presidential suite of a luxury Parisian hotel.

She couldn't understand it – Clara always knew how to get her own way because she knew what men liked, and in her experience it certainly wasn't demure smiles and apple pies.

Well, she had never failed to win and this time was bloody well not going to be any different. Aiming for the top, she had set her sights on the most powerful and influential target. Gripping the edge of her desk Clara made a solemn promise to herself. She would win this battle.

She wasn't done with Erik Danielsen yet.

8

Doubts

There were so many deliveries for Valentine's morning that Lauren had to split them between Craig in his van, Julia's little car and her own car. Between them they had worked out a schedule and by nine o'clock Lauren was at Alverston Manor with the most valuable bouquet of all. She couldn't take a chance with this many roses; they had to be delivered first thing, in the cool of the morning. An uninvited thought crept into her subconscious - would she see Greg? A small part of her hoped so.

The back door to the kitchen was ajar and she knocked tentatively. No answer. She took a deep breath and rapped on the door, much more loudly this time. A middle-aged woman hurried in response.

She beamed when she saw the mass of deep red roses. 'Ah! Beautiful, aren't they? Miss Janelle *will* be pleased!'

She damn well ought to be, Lauren mused to herself. She's got the most gorgeous man in all of Devon buying her half the roses in the country!

'I'll take them, Miss, thank you so much!'

The woman was about to close the door. Thinking quickly, Lauren asked, 'Would Mr Harrington be home? I wondered if I might ask a question.' She indicated Gretchen watching from the car window.

'Oh, you just missed him. But Miss Janelle will be here any moment, if your dog needs attention.'

'Oh, no matter – thank you anyway.' Lauren spoke quickly, feeling awkward. What was she doing? Had she taken leave of her senses? She had no question for Greg – not one she would feel comfortable asking him, at any rate – and she shouldn't waste his time. He was a busy man.

* * *

Enjoying a quiet afternoon in the shop after the rush of the Valentine's Day orders, Lauren was working on her accounts when the shop doorbell announced the arrival of a customer.

'Elaine!' Lauren smiled, delighted to unexpectedly see her friend. Gretchen got up from her basket and wagged her tail enthusiastically. 'What can I do for you?' She handed her friend a candy-pink gerbera daisy.

'Thank you.' Elaine took the bloom but did not smile. She looked unhappy, grim even, and Lauren felt a twinge of concern.

'Whatever's the matter?' she asked. Rarely had she seen her friend looking so upset.

'Lauren, look, I have something to tell you that I think you should know,' Elaine started. 'I could have called but I wanted to tell you in person.'

'This sounds serious.' Lauren pulled up a chair for Elaine to join her at the counter.

'Well, it is. You know I went to Plymouth with Reba yesterday, shopping for our dresses for the ball?'

'Yes, how did you go? Did you find what you were looking for?'

'Yes, thank you, but what I have to say is…Lauren, I am so sorry…' She trailed off, looking distressed.

'Hon, whatever is it? Surely, it can't be all that bad.' Lauren frowned with concern for her friend. She had rarely seen Elaine usually so practical and down to earth, looking so lost for words and upset.

'I don't know how to tell you.'

'Elaine, whatever it is, please – just say it!' Lauren pleaded. She was starting to imagine all kinds of dreadful scenarios.

Elaine took a deep breath and described the brief incident she'd seen with Erik and the dark-haired beauty. 'She was behaving very familiarly. They seemed to be on, well… rather *intimate* terms. I'm so sorry, Lauren.'

Lauren blinked back a few hot tears. It wasn't altogether surprising. What had she expected? What did she have to offer a man like Erik? Besides, they'd only had one proper date. 'Thank you for letting me know, she said. I had a feeling this was too good to be true. But still, it's a shame. I had dared to hope….'

'Aw, come here.' Elaine hugged Lauren close. 'You're not too upset are you? You know he's not worth losing your heart over if he doesn't appreciate what a wonderful girl you are.'

'I'll be fine. It's a disappointment, but I'll be OK.'

With a sigh, Lauren headed to the kitchen and flicked the kettle on. She didn't really want any tea, but the distraction would stop her from crying. It was just as well she had found out now that he wasn't really interested in her, before she had come to care too much.

After Elaine had gone, Lauren reached for her phone. It would be best to cancel her date with Erik.

His phone rang, but went to voicemail. She didn't feel it would be right to simply leave a message. But after the third attempt to reach him, she figured she had no choice.

'Erik, it's Lauren. I think it's best if we cancel this evening. I'll try to catch you later so we can talk.'

Oh well. Another Valentine's Day on my own. Lauren sighed as she picked up a roll of silver ribbon and began to twist it into a bow. Gretchen thumped her tail uncertainly, and settled at Lauren's feet as she worked.

Something had upset her mistress and she wasn't at all happy about it.

At five o'clock Lauren turned the key in the door and reflected on the day's events. She had always felt uneasy with the limelight. While being with Erik was fun, she had known it was likely to only be a matter of time before their differences would pull them apart – although she hadn't realised it would happen quite this quickly.

All the same, she had liked him.

Later that evening Lauren poured herself a second cup of coffee and allowed her thoughts to trail back over everything Elaine had told her. She was trying to ignore an errant tear escaping down her cheek when the shrill ring of her phone forced her back to the present.

'Hi, Laurie!' Kate's voice sang down the phone. 'Guess what?' Lauren could almost hear her sister smiling, she sounded so happy.

'Let me see… all chocolate is free now, and we are assured world peace?'

'No, silly. I got two tickets for the Charity Ball. It's a surprise for James. I was so lucky! They're selling out fast. I'm sure he'll love it! We were just saying the other day how he should come and spend a few evenings closer to my place, away from the city...' Kate babbled happily.

'OK...he doesn't actually know you have these tickets?'

'Nope. Not yet. But he'll be thrilled. I know he will!'

Lauren wasn't so sure, but she wasn't about to spoil her sister's happiness. It wouldn't hurt James Mitchell to drive out here for a change, instead of expecting Kate to fit in with his plans and his friends all the time. It was about time he treated her to a night of her choosing.

'Is Erik taking you?' Kate asked. 'You should ask him, Laurie. There's only a few tickets left - time is running out!'

'Uh...No, I don't think so. He's just...busy.'

'Are you OK? You sound upset.'

'I'm fine. No problem. Just thinking about work, you know. We've been so busy. I'm just tired, Katie, it's been a big week. But I hope you have a wonderful time, really I do.'

'Aw, I wish you two were going. If you change your mind, let me know. I am sure they would put a couple of tickets aside for you. You could collect them at the door,' Kate suggested hopefully. 'Anyhow, if I don't see you, I'll catch you later in the week. Bye for now!'

Lauren stared at her phone despondently, then decided to turn it off. She'd left Erik a message and she was damned if she was going to sit by the phone and wait for him to call. She'd speak with him tomorrow.

For now, she wanted an early night and to be left alone.

Sitting in the cool of the evening, the embers of the dying fire flickering lazily, her thoughts drifted to Greg. What was he doing tonight? Probably wining and dining Janelle, showing her how special she was to him.

With a sigh, Lauren picked up her book and settled with a blanket on the couch. She felt as if the whole world was thrilled by the excitement of life's party – to which she hadn't been invited.

* * *

Kate rifled desperately through her wardrobe. She had a vast collection of clothes, usually all carefully colour coded and immaculately hung, but were now largely strewn about her bedroom. She took pride in being neat and tidy and she had a few designer pieces that she loved. But right now, she urgently needed to find her 1940s silk chiffon ball gown in lemon and turquoise. It was beautiful. Soft and flowing, she knew the colours suited her perfectly and made her red hair glow. Excited for the night ahead, Kate had applied her make up with extra care and straightened her hair until it shone. To be honest, James had sounded less than thrilled when she called to tell him about the tickets. He sounded distant. Annoyed, even.

Maybe he was just busy, Kate thought, hurriedly fiddling with the tiny golden buckles on the ankle straps of her sandals. James was due to pick her up at seven and she didn't want to keep him waiting. Yes, that's what it was. He had just been distracted. Once he was here, they'd have a wonderful time, she was sure of it.

She was ready at seven o'clock precisely. Expecting him to knock on the door at any second, she picked up her clutch bag and checked she had everything: tickets, keys, lipstick. An excited anticipation glowed inside her. She was *so* looking forward to this ball! Some of her oldest friends would be there, and she couldn't wait to show off James to them, she was so proud of him.

Seven-ten. She glanced at her watch. He was probably held up in traffic. No matter, a few minutes wouldn't make much difference.

Kate checked her hair and makeup. She wanted to look *perfect* for James on Valentine's night. Perhaps a touch more powder on her nose. Another quick glossy layer of Cashmere Rose to her lips - there! Good to go.

A few minutes later, Kate forced herself to sit still and tried to distract herself with social media on her phone. He'd be here soon enough. What was it her mother said? 'A watched pot never boils.' Don't look at your watch and that knock on the door will come much sooner, she told herself.

Kate stole a glance at her phone. Seven twenty-five. No messages. No calls. She tried to ignore the twinge of panic inside her. Perhaps she should give him a quick call to make sure everything was OK. But she didn't want to seem pushy; he was probably on his way. Maybe she'd got the time wrong.

No. It wasn't like her to make such an absent-minded mistake. *Wait until seven-thirty,* she told herself, and tried to ignore the knot of anxiety tightening inside her. He'd be here by then… or he would send a message.

At seven-forty-five, she decided she would have to call him. She was genuinely worried. Kate pushed the call button and waited for James to pick up.

No answer.

She hung up, there was no point leaving a message. She bit her lip nervously. Perhaps something urgent had come up. Or, perhaps he was driving - though he should have shot her a message if he was going to be this late. She hoped nothing awful had happened! What if he'd had an accident?

Stop it, she told herself. *You're being silly.*

A sudden sharp knock on the door echoed through the hallway, like a summons to be obeyed.

Kate started at the sound. He was here at last. Ecstatic with relief, all anxious thoughts forgotten, Kate jumped up from the couch and hurried to fling open the door. Expecting a greeting and perhaps some cheerful banter or explanation about the delay, she smiled.

'Ready?' he asked abruptly, and turned and walked to his car.

Stunned, Kate felt as if she had been slapped, all the joyful happiness knocked out of her in an instant by his rudeness. Feeling numb with shock, she locked the door and followed him as quickly as she could. When she got to the car, he was already at the driver's seat with the engine running.

'Problems at work?' she inquired nervously, wondering what could have happened to make him so cross. Maybe a deal had gone wrong. Or something had happened on the way to her place.

'No. Well, other than having to drive out here for the evening. You know I don't like coming out here. Why couldn't we have spent the night in the city?' James glowered, and revved the car out of her driveway.

'I thought it would be a nice change. You can meet my old friends and it's going to be a good night. Besides, it's for charity. I thought it would be something different and, well, you don't come to my town very often -'

'I don't come because I don't like it!' James exclaimed. 'There's nothing out here worth going to and I don't do small town people or places, you know that. Honestly, Kate, why can't you see it's a waste of my time? We should have gone to Chansons. There's a great band playing and I had to leave to come here to suit you.'

Kate sat in shocked silence, her emotions reeling. *His* time? What about *her feelings*? She wanted to cry. To argue would be futile, she realised. She chewed her bottom lip, desperately trying to stop it from trembling and fighting to keep her distress under control. Could she have been wrong about James? She had always thought him outgoing, jovial and kind, especially towards her, but he was behaving very differently tonight. Could she have made a mistake? Misread some signal or overlooked some aspect of his personality? No, she assured herself, more than likely, something untoward had happened at the office earlier. He was just tired and stressed. She probably should have checked with him before buying the tickets. After all, she had expected him to drive all this way and do whatever she wanted without discussing it with him. Perhaps it had been a bit selfish. It would all be fine once they got there and could relax and start to enjoy their evening.

* * *

Upon their arrival at the hall, Kate couldn't help feeling a little spark of delight, despite the tense and difficult start to the evening. The impressive red, pink and white decorations were breathtaking and the music wafted along the corridor to where she stood at the entrance. The place was lively with merriment, couples heading to the main floor holding hands and laughing. Kate and James fell into step and joined them.

The solid oak doors were opened wide and two massive displays of stunning red roses on identical marble pedestals sat either side of the entrance. Kate felt a surge of excitement as they made their way to the crowded main floor. Through the crowd she could see Josh and Reba, holding hands and dancing. Reba was looking attractive in her new Chloe pastel lilac gown, which shimmered and swirled as she moved. Josh raised her hand and pulled her towards him, spinning her under his arm and taking her by surprise. He grinned and Reba laughed in delight.

Kate spotted her oldest friends from school. Excitedly, she took James's arm and ushered him along to meet them. He greeted them civilly enough, then hung his jacket on the back of her chair. As soon as politely possible he made his way to the bar with a couple of the men.

She started to relax, the distress of the earlier upset dissolving with the champagne and gaiety of the evening. It was great to catch up with her old friends, laughing and joking with them almost as if they were all back in school. Having lived in Tavistock all her life Kate felt completely at home with the friendly atmosphere and folks here. Occasionally she spied a familiar face in the crowd. Greg Harrington was there with a beautiful woman with long dark hair. She must be Janelle, his partner who had treated Gretchen last month.

Kate would have liked to dance, but James was still at the bar. No matter. She was with her crowd, girlfriends who had known her for many years. She released the disappointment of not dancing and let the music and magic of the night wash over her and soothe her soul.

Around 9 p.m. Kate heard James's phone ring. He'd left it in his jacket pocket. She ignored it at first, but it rang again. *It must be important,* she thought, and answered the call. The caller hung up.

Strange, Kate thought and glanced at the screen. Cynthia? From the office? Why would she be calling James? And she'd called more than once. It must be something to do with work. They were obviously working on a case together. Kate shrugged and dropped the phone into the inside pocket of his jacket. Work could take a back seat tonight. She'd tell him later that Cynthia had called.

As night descended and the evening came to a close, people started to drift away and Kate and her friends collected their belongings to leave.

'Come on,' said James, sounding irritated. 'It's getting late and I have to drive back to the city.' He turned away from her and started towards the door.

'OK. I'm ready. I'll just get my coat. Oh, by the way, Cynthia called you.'

'What?' He spun back to her, his expression hard as steel.

'Your phone rang. I couldn't see you at the bar, so I answered it.' She slipped her arms into her coat. 'I was going to take a message, but she hung up before I could—'

'You answered my phone?' James's eyes flashed with anger. 'I'll thank you not to touch my phone. *Ever!* Who do you think you are? My secretary?'

'I'm sorry, I didn't think—'

'That's precisely the problem, isn't it, Kate?' he fired at her, his face like thunder. 'You just *don't think.* What in heaven's name made you assume I would want to come out here tonight to this place? We could have gone to any of the clubs or bars in the city, but instead I had to come all the way out here to please you.'

'You didn't have to!' Kate cried in dismay. 'If you really didn't want to come, then you shouldn't have. No one *forced* you. I thought it would be a nice thing for us to do together. But if you hate it here so much, then you *shouldn't have come!'*

A hard lump filled her throat and hot tears threatened to spill down her cheeks. What was wrong? Why was he so angry?

Miserably, she sank into the soft leather of the luxury car seat, her arms folded across her chest, trying to make herself as small as she felt. She steeled herself for the long ride home, confusion and upset washing over her.

He never used to be this way. A tear slid down her cheek but she was too proud to brush it away and let James see her crying. She must be doing something wrong.

But what it was, and how to correct it and put things right between them, Kate had no idea.

9

Truth

'Lauren?' Erik's voice sounded uncharacteristically uncertain. 'I just got your message. I don't understand. Is everything OK?'

No. Lauren cringed inside. Everything certainly wasn't bloody well OK. As much as she didn't want to have this conversation, she needed to be open and honest with him. She took a deep breath.

'If you're free tonight, I can meet you.'

Better face him and get this whole ridiculous pretence over with, preferably somewhere public but quiet. She suggested a small, pleasant bar nearby and was pleased he agreed.

As planned, she arrived at seven and was about to push the door open when she heard a familiar voice behind her.

'Allow me.' Erik opened the door for her.

'Thank you.' Lauren kept her voice civil but cool.

They chose a quiet table and Erik held the chair for her. Always the gentleman, she thought ruefully. It was one of the things she liked about him.

'What can I get you to drink?' he asked.

'Nothing, thank you.'

He frowned in concern. 'Lauren, what's wrong? Has something upset you?'

Lauren stared at him. Where to start?

A waiter came over to take their order, but Erik waved him away.

'OK, tell me what's bothering you,' he said, his voice like silk.

How could he be so convincingly smooth? Surely he must know by now that she wasn't the sort of woman who was casual about relationships. He wasn't stupid!

'Look, Erik, I came here to tell you I appreciate the dates and the lovely times we have shared but I know all good things must come to an end.' She ignored his puzzled look. 'It's OK, I completely understand–'

Erik leaned back in his chair and shook his head. 'Well, I am glad one of us does!'

'Let's not play games. It's obvious we are worlds apart and want and expect different things from a relationship. It's been great, really it has, but I can't be in a relationship unless it's exclusive and I think it's only fair–'

'Wait! What?' Erik looked genuinely confused. 'Lauren, what do you mean? Has someone said something to you?'

'Not so much what they said as what they *saw.*' Lauren was unable to keep the indignation and hurt from her voice. Why was he making this so difficult? She bit hard on her lower lip to stop it from trembling. She had to keep it together.

'Now you're being cryptic. Lauren, if someone has said something to you then let me know exactly what they saw – or *thought* they saw, please.'

Lauren took a deep breath to try and dislodge the strangling feeling around her chest that had now risen to her throat. She explained what Elaine had seen.

Erik listened carefully throughout. Then he leaned back in his chair, as if digesting the information. His blue eyes darkened.

'So, your friend saw me with a woman and you both assumed I must be seeing her romantically?' His words were sharp and deliberate, hard like flint.

It was Lauren's turn to be puzzled.

'Well, yes, I suppose…it certainly seemed that way.' Lauren faltered.

Erik placed both hands on the arms of his chair and, holding her gaze, stood and went to the bar. Lauren stared after him. How dare he leave her sitting there like that, with no explanation? What was he thinking? She sat fuming in stony silence, biting harder on her lip.

Within minutes he returned with two drinks and carefully placed a glass of wine in front of her before taking his seat opposite. His eyes had softened and there was a slight crease of anxiety in his forehead.

'Lauren,' he began, speaking slowly and carefully. 'A considerable part of my job is to be charming. I have to meet influential representatives of the wealthiest companies in the world – and run a company successfully. I am responsible for the overall performance of Clarence and Fulton and I have to be available to clients, partners and my team as they need me. Everyone makes demands. Some clients are special and exceptionally valuable. We have to prove we can handle all their policy requirements, however demanding or complicated they might be.' His voice was warm, smooth and soothing like molten caramel. 'I cannot do all this alone.'

'So, that woman Elaine saw you with…'

'That was Clara Beaufort. My second-in-command. I rely on her to work with me on some of the more complicated and time-consuming cases.' Clara. Lauren recalled the stunning beauty she'd seen at Chansons on the evening of her birthday. 'We met some potential new clients from Prague for lunch. Afterwards, I spent the afternoon with her going through statistics and contracts. She can be charming and she's certainly stunning, but it's strictly business as far as I am concerned. It has to be. Either James or I deal with the female clients while Clara deals with the males. It's the nature of the beast. It just works better that way.'

That made perfect sense, Lauren reasoned. From what she'd learned so far, it would be very difficult for any man to say no to Clara Beaufort.

'Erik, I am sorry. Of course I can see the need for both of you to meet clients. It just sounded so…*personal.*'

'No, not personal,' Erik said. 'Professional as far as I am concerned, I promise you. I won't lie to you, Lauren, if it seals the deal we are after, I will work closely with anyone I have to. The client has to come first and I have to make sure my staff are happy and well looked after too. That way they are more productive – if people feel appreciated, they work harder. But it's all left at the office. Everyone understands that. I have had my fair share of shallow, superficial relationships that just don't seem to go anywhere. Dead-ends and false starts. I have spent enough time looking for someone smart, kind and independent, someone with a true heart that I can trust and share special moments with.'

His smile melted her heart as he reached for her hand, his

touch reassuring. 'I wanted to be with you because I felt I could relate to you, trust you. I chose you because I could see something special in you.'

Conflicting emotions stirred deep inside Lauren. She felt as if she had slipped between two difficult paths, one steep and challenging, the other confusing and twisting.

She was fond of Erik. He had been good to her. Yet his love of the city lifestyle and his demanding business ideals were so different from her own dreams.

'So, Miss Sinclair,' Erik teased, looking serious and leaning in towards her in a conspiratorial manner that made her heart jump with anticipation. 'Can you see that? Can you understand what being with me may mean?'

'Thank you for being so honest with me.' She faltered. His intensity made her breathless and she was dizzy with all the information.

She sipped her wine and sat back in her chair, but was far from relaxed.

It was clear that Erik was tired of glamorous but shallow relationships and was genuinely interested in her. He was also supremely confident and a natural leader, head of an important company in the city and used to getting what he wanted. But this could be dangerous for her – and she wasn't at all sure it could work between them. They were from different worlds with conflicting ideas about what an idyllic lifestyle and happiness meant.

This was as clear to her as the flawless cut glass crystal on their table. She had some serious thinking to do.

10

An Anniversary

Clara pressed her back into the cool leather of her office chair and massaged the back of her neck. She'd spent the morning locked in intense conversation with major league French clients who had now decided they would like to 'take time to peruse' her proposals.

Typical of Friday the thirteenth. She might have known everything would go wrong today.

'Sod this. I need a drink.'

Pushing away from her desk, she stood and reached for her bag and jacket. Erik had been missing for the best part of the afternoon and she had held the fort, worked with the French company and dealt with numerous phone inquiries. She'd had enough. Slipping her jacket over her shoulders, she beckoned to Cynthia. If she was going to leave the office early, it would look official if she took a colleague with her.

Cynthia's puzzled expression quickly turned to understanding and she eagerly grabbed her coat and bag. Together they slipped out of the office and made their way to the elevator. Fortunately, Cynthia knew better than to pry on the way down to the street.

'Where to?' she asked when they stepped out of the building into the mid-afternoon bustle of the city. 'Chansons?'

'No, not Chansons. We might be seen. Somewhere away from this place.' She was entitled to a break but it wouldn't do to draw attention to the fact they'd left work early. 'Maybe… Pilgrims.' It was quieter, on the edge of town and a bit of peace and sanity was exactly what she needed.

They managed to get a cab almost straight away. Through the window she watched as the heavy city traffic gradually thinned and a sense of calm crept over her. Soon they reached their destination and were heading into the warmth of an aging grey stone building. The sound of hushed voices and a faint smell of hops and smoke drifted towards them as Clara led the way to the bar. They ordered and headed for a booth near the fire.

She sipped her drink and sank thankfully into the faux leather bench seat. 'It's good to get out of that place.'

Cynthia nodded. She stared around them, taking in the dimly lit shabbiness of the decor. 'Clara, are you OK? I mean, we don't usually come here -'

'I know. I just needed a change.' She wasn't about to admit it to Cynthia but Erik's evasiveness lately had affected her mood and concentration at work. If only she knew how to win him over. Surely there must be a way?

'Look, Cynthia, this morning when you were going through the client appointments with Maria she didn't happen to mention where Erik was today, did she?'

'Nope, sorry. Not a clue. I just got a million orders from that bossy bitch about what she thinks I need to do next week.'

'Hmm. Well, when he gets back, he'll have some explaining to do. Want another drink?'

Cynthia shook her head. 'Not for me, thanks.'

'I'm getting one.'

When Clara returned, Cynthia picked up the conversation.

'Men. They're a pain, right? There's this guy at work I *really* like, we're going to this new place in town tomorrow, Vagabonds it's called. You should come. It looks great. But honestly, he's so wrapped up with this little idiot at the office. No experience, I honestly don't know why Erik trusted her with the Mulberry Park case when I could have done it so much better – are you OK?'

'Of course. Something in my eye, that's all.' She quickly crumpled the tissue and thrust it into her bag, then reached for her drink.

'Are you sure?'

'I said I'm *OK*,' Clara snapped. She took a long swallow of her drink and then forced a smile. 'It's just not a good day for me.'

'If it's important, I can try to find out where Erik is. I'll ask Maria, pretend I have some burning questions I need to ask...'

'No, it's fine. If I need him, I can get hold of him. Thanks though.' She stared into her drink. 'To be honest, it's not just him. There's other trials. Like I said, it's a bad time right now.'

'Well, if I can help, just say the word.'

'You can't. No one can.' Clara's lip trembled and she gripped her glass tightly as she took another swallow. The double vodka and lime was going down well and soothed the lump in her throat. But, to her shame, a hot tear trickled down her cheek and another threatened to escape. She took a deep breath, rose to her feet and pushed in her chair. She'd best make for the ladies, get herself under control.

'Clara…'

Too late. Cynthia had noticed. It was no good trying to pretend she wasn't crying. Clara slumped back down and managed a strangled laugh.

'It's not what you think. It's not Erik.'

'I wasn't. I mean, I didn't think…'

'It's my sister. I lost my sister ten years ago today.' Even speaking the words was a weight crushing through from her chest to her spine.

'Oh! I didn't know….I mean….I'm so sorry.' Cynthia stammered, her face a picture of compassion. 'I didn't know you had a sister. What happened? I mean, you can tell me, if you like.'

Clara took another swallow of her drink. She had to get a grip. This was madness. She never shared the secrets of her past, especially with colleagues. Why start now? But as the alcohol soothed its way into her psyche, she sat back and looked steadily through the haze of tears at her friend. It would be good to talk. She rarely did. She took a deep breath and found herself recanting past events as clearly as if they had happened yesterday.

'She was my twin. My best friend. We lived in the countryside, and there wasn't much to do really. One weekend, there was a dance in the town. Nothing exciting ever happened in our sleepy village. We both really wanted to go, but our father wouldn't let us. Said we had to stay home and study. He had a real temper, especially when he drank. But Paulette had a boyfriend and he said he'd take her and damn the old man. He stole his father's car to drive them there.' Clara took another deep swallow of her drink, her soft French accent slurring her words slightly.

'Our older brother Jacques went with them. They were so excited and they made me promise not to tell anyone they were going. Paulette looked lovely.' Clara bowed her head as she remembered the new dress her sister had made, her excitement and spirited laughter at the chance to escape the drudgery for a night. Clara had been jealous, but she hadn't dared go. She knew full well the price to be paid for upsetting their father. Their mother had borne the full force of his anger many times.

'She knew about our father's rages but was determined to be with her love. She was sick of staying at home, and she was much braver than me.'

Clara paused at the pain of her memories, crystal clear and wounding her soul.

'On the way home, at two in the morning, her boyfriend lost control of the car and crashed into a tree. In that instant I lost my sister and my brother. My world was changed forever.'

'Oh my God, Clara, I am *so sorry!*' Cynthia instinctively reached across the table for Clara's hand, but then thought better of it. 'I had no idea.'

Clara was silent, her face drained of colour, caught in the memory of the unbearable pain of loss and the dark days that followed.

'It must have been so terrible for you. How did you bear it?'

'I worked hard. Studied hard. My mother was useless with grief and never managed to break free from depression. My father suffered post-traumatic stress and spent his days drinking in the local tavern, only coming home to eat, sleep and drunkenly abuse what was left of his family. I hated them both and promised myself I would get out as soon as I could. I got my first class degree at Avignon University and came to London.'

She didn't mention the kind-hearted, diligent young man with dreams of owning his own property development business who had accompanied her to London, or the way she'd left him behind without a backward glance when she scored her dream job with Clarence and Fulton. Nothing and nobody was ever going to get in the way of her dreams or hurt her again. This was *her* opportunity, *her* turn to shine, *her* future in the making. One look at her new boss Erik Danielson had confirmed this was where she *belonged*.

11

A Shock

The sound of the front door closing and Chester's happy welcome bark heralded Shirley's arrival. 'Hi! I'm back!' her voice shrilled through the hallway. 'Ready for lunch? I thought we could go to the Rose Garden café in town.'

'Kate's just on the phone, Mum,' Lauren mouthed, pointing to the kitchen. 'James called. Not sure what he wants, but she's been on the phone for a few minutes now.'

'OK. I'll just get ready upstairs and then we'll be away. Hope everything is all right,' Shirley added in a hushed tone. James could become annoyed if Kate didn't agree with his plans.

'I don't know.'

Through the closed door of the sitting room, Lauren could hear her sister's muffled voice saying, 'I am sorry... I just don't think... No, James, that's not it at all... I just need a little time to finish the Mulberry Park case...'

A few minutes later, Kate emerged looking a little shaken. 'Everything OK?' Lauren asked.

'I don't know, really. I've upset James. He wanted us to meet his friends at a new place in the city this afternoon, but I am so tired after work all week and I promised you and Mum we'd go to lunch. I hate arguing with him. I just wish he'd understand.'

'Oh, Kate, he should understand if you have plans and are tired. I don't know what his problem is.'

'It's my fault,' Kate said sadly. 'I should try to fit in with his friends and his plans more. Perhaps he feels I'm not making enough effort.'

'Nonsense!' Lauren retorted. 'He shouldn't be so possessive of you. You work hard, you're entitled to relax with your family at the weekend. He should understand that. You could meet him another evening. Or he could come here to see you. He doesn't often do that.'

'I told him I couldn't make it today, but maybe I made a mistake,' Kate said uncertainly. 'He's busy and there's more to do in the city. He doesn't really like coming out to the country. I expect he'll come out to us soon. I hope so. I don't like annoying him and lately I seem to be upsetting him all the time.'

'It doesn't seem to take much. Besides, you shouldn't be at his beck and call. He could just as easily come and join us. It wouldn't hurt him to make a little effort for you.'

At that moment Shirley appeared from upstairs and gave Lauren a questioning look to ask if all was OK with Kate. Lauren shook her head but mouthed, 'Not now.' Kate was clearly upset. Best to let the subject go for now.

'All set,' she said instead and, linking arms with her mother and sister, headed for her car.

The air was crisp and clear, and the snow had gone, melting

into grey slush and then quickly disappearing, leaving shiny wet pavements as a reminder. Shirley had chosen a pretty little café in a quiet area of town, away from the hustle and bustle of busy Duke Street. In the golden warmth of the café, she pushed her menu aside and studied her younger daughter. She had seen so little of Kate since her promotion and she worried for her. Kate had an excellent work ethic and had always tackled any project with commitment and enthusiasm. Shirley knew she would be one of the first to arrive and the last to leave the office, always conscientious, always meticulous with details and doing the best she possibly could. But she had never seen her looking so tired and worn out. Tell-tale dark circles had appeared under her eyes and she was sure Kate had lost weight.

Concern prompted her to ask. 'Kate dear, are you quite well?' 'Not overdoing it at work? How's your new project going?'

'Great!' Kate enthused. 'I love having the Mulberry Park caseload to myself. I am almost done, the deadline is the end of next week. I've basically got their policies in place, worked out to their specific requirements and I just need to fine-tune the details. It's been *a lot* of work, but I *know* I can do it. Once it's finished we'll go out and celebrate!'

Shirley wasn't convinced by the bright smile or cheerful manner, but didn't pursue it during lunch. As soon as they had finished eating, Kate decided to go to the city and meet James after all.

'Be safe!' Lauren warned and hugged her close. 'Drive carefully. I know you're tired.'

'I will,' she promised.

Shirley and Lauren watched her leave, then ordered coffee

and settled into the comfortable chairs near a small open fireplace.

'I am worried about that girl,' Shirley said.

'I know, Mum,' Lauren agreed. 'She looks so tired and she *always* puts James first before her own needs. Honestly, Mum, he should understand she's had extra pressure at work. He's not exactly helping – he's just adding to her stress.'

'Yes, but what can we do? It's her life and she loves him. I feel all I can do is support her and be there for both of you when you need me.'

Lauren reached over and gave her mother's arm a squeeze. 'We know that,' she smiled. 'I'll look out for her as best I can. Our Katie will be OK. She's a big girl now.'

* * *

The truth was, Kate had never felt so tired, and the evenings she spent working to pull the Mulberry Park case together had irritated James, who demanded more and more of her attention on her few days off. When she first met him he had been jovial, outgoing and attentive. She had never had such a good-looking and popular boyfriend. A natural leader, James loved to be the centre of attention, always at the most fashionable events and locations, surrounded by friends. It had been fun, and she had felt flattered and lucky to have his attention.

But recently the pressure to keep up with his plans, ideas and socialising was wearing her down. Lauren thought he was possessive, but Kate wouldn't have described him like that. But his behaviour had changed recently. Could he be a little jealous of her success since her promotion? No, surely not. He was missing her, that's all. She'd meet him in the city and surprise him and everything would be fine.

As she drove, Kate smiled happily. She was on her way to meet James and she loved him and everything would be perfect again in her world.

* * *

Unaccustomed to arriving anywhere alone, Kate tentatively pushed open the door to Vagabonds and paused at the entrance, needing a few seconds to get her bearings and for her eyes to adjust to the dark. She blinked once or twice and heard James's booming laughter to the side of the room. Looking to her right, she saw a slim girl in a short skirt holding a glass and leaning on a man. Cynthia! She hadn't realised Cynthia had a boyfriend. Well, good for her! She was glad for her, relieved even – perhaps she might be nicer to work with now.

Cynthia had her arm wrapped around her boyfriend's back, caressing his neck, and as Kate watched, she leaned in close and whispered to him. The whispers turned into a passionate kiss and Kate smiled as she began to walk towards the group. New love! The man gave Cynthia's bottom a suggestive squeeze, then lifted his head and laughed.

No! It couldn't be!

Shock halted Kate, freezing her movements. An icy cold stone sank to the pit of her stomach.

James. *Her* James. With Cynthia.

Waves of pain seared through her body like glass shards, shredding her heart and leaving her raw inside. She couldn't breathe and her legs threatened to give way. She clutched the doorframe for support. A sob escaped as she leaned against it, and James turned. His smile didn't falter but his eyes widened in recognition.

Cynthia followed his gaze and her look of surprise changed to a triumphant smirk in an instant.

Kate turned, blinded by her tears, and ran out of the building.

12

Realisation

Monday morning the alarm went off at five - thirty. Kate swung her legs wearily over the side of the bed. She hadn't slept well, tossing and turning with anxiety about James's betrayal drifting through her mind and into her dreams. It was early and pale silvery morning light peeked through her blinds into the gloom of the bedroom. She stood up, yawned and stretched. Suddenly, her necklace snapped and fell to the floor, an explosion of red jasper beads bouncing on and around her feet. In dismay Kate watched them roll all over the floor and under her bed. Clearly her favourite healing crystal necklace had absorbed all the anxiety and tension it could manage.

Probably saturated with it, Kate thought miserably. *Great. What a fantastic start to the week.*

There had been a ridiculous phone call from James, who had blamed everyone and everything – the bar, the barman, the drink, the situation, Cynthia, his friends and even Kate herself. Kate had been tempted to let the whole thing slide and give him a second chance until her sense of reason and self-respect kicked in; he would probably do this again and besides, how would she be able to trust him now? She couldn't, Kate told herself for the millionth time. They had promised to keep their distance from each other as far as practically possible at work – it shouldn't be too difficult. James was an agent. Kate worked in sales. He could easily go to other members of her team. She needn't deal with him directly. It was better this way.

Clean break. Forget him. Move on.

Kate went about her early morning routine on autopilot.

Jog. Shower. Hair. Emails. Makeup. Purse. Bag. Car keys.

A beautiful sunrise driving over the moors lifted her spirits momentarily; perhaps there were brighter things on the horizon for her. Arriving early at the office, she was surprised to find she was the only person there. Not even Erik had arrived yet. No matter, Kate was too numb to care. She switched on her computer, fetched a latte, put her head down and started working.

Her latte cold and untouched, she barely noticed when Erik arrived and unintentionally ignored his greeting. The others drifted in around nine and the office vibe picked up with the low hum of subdued voices and occasional laughter.

Kate paid little attention to what was going on around her. She was determined not to let James see how upset she was. Nor anyone else here. She'd got this. She could do it. All would be well as long as he kept his distance as promised. *Work,* she told herself.

Don't think, don't analyse. Just work.

Lunchtime came and went. Kate remained at her desk. At three o'clock Erik delivered a latte to her desk and touched her lightly on the shoulder. Kate looked up in surprise, grateful to find he already had his back turned and was walking away when she felt hot tears welling at his kind gesture.

At four Kate received an email from him. 'Astounding work today. I appreciate your effort. Go home early today, Kate. You deserve it – you haven't stopped all day!'

As she stuffed her belongings into her bag and stood to leave, Kate realised she was exhausted and was glad of an early reprieve. All she wanted was a hot bath and an early night. She glanced at Erik's office. He nodded and she left without saying a word to anyone, unable to shake the leaden burden in her heart.

Driving home over the moors, she couldn't help the tears from spilling down her cheeks and onto her jacket. Emotionally, she was eggshell fragile.

Would she *ever* feel better?

* * *

Lauren wasn't often unwell but this morning she woke to a swirling cloud of pain behind her eyes that threatened to turn into a migraine and her throat felt like she had swallowed sand paper in her sleep. Determined to shake it off and get on with her day, she forced herself to sit up and shift her legs wearily over the side of the bed – then promptly lay down again, overcome by dizziness. Waves of nausea swept over her, her head felt stuffed with cotton wool and she couldn't think clearly.

There was no way she could work today. She called the shop and told Julia to do her best without her, then spent the morning dozing. Gretchen instinctively understood her mistress needed peace and quiet and rested her head in her

Lauren's lap.

Craig turned up at midday with Buddy to take Gretchen out in the van with him on the afternoon deliveries so at least she would have a walk and a play in the park. He even brought Buddy along so they could have a game in the park together. After they left Lauren remembered she was supposed to be going out with Erik that evening. *Well,* she thought sadly, *there's no way I can get dressed and made up and drive to Plymouth for a night out tonight. I can barely summon the energy to make it from the couch to the kitchen! What a shame.* She had been looking forward to the evening. She left a message for him and took herself back into bed.

By six o'clock, after a hot shower with a floral scented gel, two Paracetamol and a change into crisp white pyjamas covered with red rosebuds, Lauren was feeling a little better. Face scrubbed clean and freshly washed hair piled loosely on top of her head, she was lounging on the couch with a mug of hot lemon tea with honey, waiting for Craig to bring Gretchen home.

Hearing an engine pull up outside, she assumed it was Craig, and waited for him to push the door open and let Gretchen in. But no excited puppy bounded in, eager to see her mistress. Lauren got up from the couch and peered through the drawn curtains.

Oh no! It can't be!

A wave of panic swept over her at the sight of the gleaming silver-grey Maserati in her driveway. Lauren took a deep breath to control her panic, hastily smoothed wisps of stray hair and reached for the door handle.

Erik filled the doorway, holding an expensive looking bottle of claret and a colourful mixed bouquet. 'Forgive me,

I don't mean to intrude but I just wanted to see you and wish you better soon.'

'Oh, Erik, that's so sweet of you!' Lauren said, flustered. 'And so thoughtful. Would you like to come in?'

'Thank you, if you're sure you feel well enough, maybe for a few minutes.'

He was about to step over the threshold when Lauren froze in horror. A muddy blur of gigantic proportions came bounding gleefully up the driveway, red drooling tongue lolling.

Oh, this couldn't be...

'Buddy!' yelled Craig. 'Buddy! Come back!'

With joyful abandon, Buddy recognised his friend Lauren and pounded up to say hello.

'Buddy! Nooo!'

At Lauren's horrified expression, Erik spun round. There was no time to escape the onslaught. He pushed Lauren safely to one side and braced himself to protect her. Buddy launched himself at this new friend who was clearly up for a fun game of wrestling. Showering Erik with mud and water, he planted two wet plate-sized paws on the breast of his designer jacket. Behind Buddy, Gretchen started to bark anxiously.

Lauren didn't know whether to laugh or cry. This clearly wasn't the reception Erik had expected: her standing in the doorway in her pyjamas while he gallantly fought off the slobbering beast of a dog to the tune of deafening barking, all the while armed with a bottle of wine and flowers.

Poor Erik.

Over the mess and din, Lauren grabbed the glass bottle for safety's sake before Erik was tempted to crack Buddy on the head with it. Shooting Craig a pained look when he finally managed to grab his dog by the collar, she tugged Erik into the hallway by his sleeve, let Gretchen in and then quickly slammed the door.

Flushed, breathing heavily and completely dishevelled, Erik regained his composure and presented Lauren with the tattered bouquet.

Fighting to keep a straight face, she graciously accepted it.

'What in heaven's name was that?' exclaimed Erik.

'That would be Buddy, otherwise known as the Beast of Dartmoor. Let me make you a hot drink, or would you like something stronger?' Lauren looked him up and down. 'Perhaps you'd like to clean up a bit first. Come. The bathroom is this way...'

* * *

Half an hour later, the worst of the mess had been cleaned up and they had a hot mug of tea each. Erik had been stripped of his ruined jacket, with promises of getting it to a specialist dry cleaner the next day. He was now relaxed, with the sleeves of his crisp shirt rolled up, brilliant white against his smooth tanned skin.

'Charming,' he said taking in Lauren's place and complimented her on the tasteful furnishings and décor. But he was clearly less comfortable with the watchful German Shepherd in the room. Gretchen had tried nuzzling his hand affectionately, her favourite trick with new friends, but he had jumped up from the sofa and taken long strides to the opposite side of the room. Unsettled by this reaction, she had retreated uncertainly to her basket next to Lauren.

'It's OK, she won't hurt you,' Lauren said, bending down to fondle Gretchen's head.

'I don't like dogs,' Erik explained. 'I never did, not even

as a child.'

'Perhaps you are more of a cat person?'

'Not really. I'm allergic to them.'

'Not a pet person at all then?'

'No,' he agreed throwing her one of his charming smiles and turned the conversation to their common interest in music.

He didn't stay late, explaining he thought she probably needed rest more than company.

Later, Lauren put her book aside and lay in bed considering the evening's events. She liked Erik. She really did. He was intelligent, smart, sexy and – evidently – very brave. After all, he had tried to protect her against the Beast of Dartmoor, not knowing Buddy was a big softie.

But Lauren didn't think she could love him. They were too different and their ideals and expectations were not the same. It was if there was a great chasm between them that would never be filled.

In the peace and stillness of her bedroom, Lauren reflected on their differences. Why was she so self-conscious in the public eye? Erik was so relaxed and at ease in the limelight. Could she seriously see herself being with someone who couldn't bear to be near her beloved Gretchen? Did she want to change her whole lifestyle, move away from the place she loved and live in the city? Where could this lead and what future, if any, was there in a relationship like this?

There was no conceivable way she would ever lie to him, or to herself. He deserved better. What was it her grandmother used to say? Words from her childhood rang clear in her memory. 'To thine own self be true'.

Regretfully, Lauren sighed as she leaned to switch off her bedroom lamp. Her head was full of questions but in the darkness of her bedroom, she was sure of one thing. She and Erik were over.

13

A Perfect Gentleman

Cynthia leaned back in her chair idly flicking through emails and tapping short, purple manicured fingernails on the desk. She should have been working on the sales statistics but had quickly become bored and distracted. She would do them later, when the final figures for the entire week were available. Besides it was more interesting to think about James.

He had told her she should apply for a new position in sales, so she decided to work on her resume. She wanted a better position; she was tired of taking orders and being pushed around. Flicking open her personal documents file and started reading, absentmindedly chewing a fingernail. Prior to joining Clarence and Fulton she had attended university. Well, that much was true. Her parents had paid for her to go - her father had worked extra hours in his car dealership business to make the money, and she knew he was proud she had taken a place. Cynthia could always twist him around her little finger.

What had she achieved *outside* of work? Well…not

much. Her father had always called her 'his Princess' but she couldn't very well put that down. As a child she has been given anything she wanted, literally *anything* - she only had to ask for it. Dolls, clothes, toys, books and then later it was makeup, jewellery, concert tickets and parties.

Her mind drifted back to James. Knowing he was taken had not stopped her making a play for him. He was good looking, well connected and popular and she was drawn to successful people. It was easier to get ahead if you made the right friends.

She wished she could boast she'd gained a first class degree. Something that sounded exceptional. Perhaps she could bend the truth a little, but she hadn't really applied herself at university. She couldn't be bothered with the assignments and quickly fell behind with the coursework. The only part of student life that interested her was the social calendar and if it hadn't been for her Mark, her kind and gentle boyfriend at the time, she would not have achieved her degree at all. He had given up most evenings and weekends to help her pass the final exams, but by the time she had graduated, Cynthia had grown bored with him. He had outlived his usefulness, so she left him as well as two months rent in advance and the fees for her online tuition on his credit card to remember her by.

Cynthia had worked for a few different companies and had met Clara at her last job. They had become allies; and Cynthia's father had helped Clara buy a new BMW sports coupe at a very good price. When Clara had left and gained a senior position at Clarence and Fulton she had suggested Cynthia apply to join the sales team. Cynthia had jumped at the chance - the pay was better, the work easier and there was a decent social agenda.

Plus, she got to be near that gorgeous, famous rich guy who was in charge. But, so far, he hadn't even noticed her. She removed her glasses and rubbed her eyes. She doubted Erik even knew her name. Never mind, she consoled herself. James Marshall would do.

At least, he would do for *now*.

It was Kate's own fault she had lost him. She wasn't worthy of a man like James. He needed someone attentive, appreciative, who would support him and go along with his plans and schemes, not someone who wanted her own portfolio and who was always too busy to put him first. Cynthia had been there for him when he needed her. Kate hadn't. He was alone in that bar in Plymouth and as far as she was concerned, it had been a simple case of 'finders keepers, losers weepers.'

A new email bounced onto the screen from Erik's assistant, Maria. She quickly replaced her glasses. What was this? Something about going out for drinks on Friday night. For *exceeding their quota*....and celebrate that bloody Kate's success with her stupid Mulberry Park case! Cynthia started at the screen in disbelief, bitter bile rising up into the back of her throat. A jealous rage silently built up inside her, she gripped the arms of her chair until her knuckles were white.

The Mulberry Park portfolio should have been hers. She'd handled so many projects like that in her previous employment, loads more than Kate Sinclair. Clara had done her best to get the portfolio assigned to Cynthia but bloody Erik had overridden her and given it to Kate. It was ludicrous to let such a junior nobody take it on and Cynthia had hoped she'd fail. Clara had said not to worry, Kate was bound to screw it up. But here they were, about to have drinks to celebrate Kate's success.

Well, she'd just have to see about that.

* * *

Kate looked despondently out of the taxi window at the blur of coloured windows as she zipped through the city streets. The last thing she felt like doing was getting dressed up and heading out on her own to Chansons.

Recently, she had found it hard to muster a degree of enthusiasm for anything other than hard work. When she was absorbed in her work, nothing else mattered. There was simply no room for negative emotions, or harking back over sad memories. It was as if she were a blank canvas, the only marks fresh and new, made in the here and now. Nothing from the past. Nothing from the future. Just the present, that very moment, mattered.

Nervously, she chewed her bottom lip and stared out of the window at the early nightlife unfolding on the streets. She felt a knot of apprehension work its tangled way through her insides. She wasn't used to being alone and missed the good times she had with James. She smoothed the crisp dark burgundy material of her 1950s vintage ball dress, the latest addition to her wardrobe. She'd refashioned it and pressed it to fit perfectly and it was immaculate, like new. To occupy herself, she snapped open her powder compact and checked her reflection, and applied a layer of frosty pink lipstick, which glistened like glacé icing.

The taxi stopped outside the wine bar and Kate found herself standing alone, bathed in the soft yellow glow from the entrance. Echoes of laughter and music drifted into the street. Kate stared at the closed door in front of her. It had been a favourite spot, glamorous and hip, and previously she had loved the party atmosphere. It felt strange to be here now in such a familiar place but alone. Surreal.

She took a deep breath to summon up her inner courage.

Oh well. Here goes. If James or Cynthia were here, she'd just have to deal with it.

Sod it. Sod both of them.

This was *her* night as much as anyone's. She had every right – *more* than that – to be here tonight. She wasn't going to let them spoil her success. Smiling as brightly as she could manage, she pushed open the door and forced herself through a portal into a world of warmth, jazz and laughter.

'Hi Kate!' Erik appeared and took her hand.

Grateful for his attention, she kissed him lightly in greeting and followed him to join her colleagues at their table. Smiling apprehensively, she was relieved to find James and Cynthia weren't there. Soon she was enjoying herself, chatting happily to colleagues; she even danced a little and, after drinking enough chardonnay to feel agreeably dizzy, was surprised to hear herself openly laugh for the first time in weeks. She felt supported, buoyed up by the appreciation and energy of those around her.

Towards the end of the evening, Erik leaned towards her and took her hand. 'Dance?'

'Sure, why not?' she agreed happily and they headed to the dance floor, Erik confidently leading her through a sea of couples, all gyrating in time to the lively, cheerful beat. She had an unexpectedly good time. Actually, she'd had a *great* time. She smiled appreciatively at Erik.

As the evening drew to a close and people drifted towards the street, Erik offered to give her a lift home.

'Really, it's OK - I'll get a taxi...' Kate started to protest, but let herself be led to the door.

Outside, she pulled her coat around her tightly to keep out the chill of the night air and fell into an easy pace by his side. They approached a group of people, rowdy with drink, shouting exuberantly at each other in some argument and he slipped his arm around her shoulders protectively.

Reaching his car, Erik opened the door for her and she slipped inside, grateful for the safety and warmth.

Minutes later, Kate was sitting outside her apartment block thanking Erik for a great night – really it had been better than she could have imagined.

'Glad you came?' He smiled at kindly at her. 'I had a feeling you could perhaps do with a little cheering up just lately.'

'Yes, very glad. Thanks Erik. It was just what I needed!'

'Good. Well, you know where I am if you need me. I'll see you Monday. Enjoy the rest of your weekend!'

He waited until she was safely in the building, then Kate saw the sleek car drive smoothly away, out of view.

Such a nice guy, Kate thought happily. Laurens' words echoed in her memory.

'A perfect gentleman.'

14

Confusion

K ate stared at the blank screen in disbelief. She was having the day from Hell. One of those inexplicably frustrating days where nothing, absolutely nothing, would go right.

This morning she had lost a major contract that she had spent weeks chasing and perfecting for wealthy but difficult engineering clients Brooke and Co. That had annoyed Erik, but these things happened. She couldn't explain why; they had been extremely picky but she had met every demand. It should have been a straightforward enough deal.

Two important blue plastic files containing data she had diligently worked on had mysteriously gone missing from her desk; and now her computer had crashed.

Dammit.

What a morning. What else could go wrong? She ran her hand through her hair as she rocked back in her chair.

'*Kate!*' a male voice cut sharply into her thoughts.

She looked up, straight into her boss's angry face.

'Kate, what time were the French clients booked for?' Erik

thundered, his mouth a grim line, his eyes dark as flint.

Stunned, Kate thought swiftly. She had organised an important meeting with six representatives of a large, prestigious French firm for Erik that afternoon.

'2 p.m. as you asked,' she smiled, hoping to dispel the tension. She had never seen Erik looking so angry.

'Then why the bloody hell are they all here, expecting me to see them at 11 a.m?' Erik roared at her.

Oh. My. God. Major *disaster.*

How could she have screwed this up? Panic rose from the pit of her stomach.

'Oh, Erik, I am so sorry, I must have sent the wrong time,' she whimpered. Though how it had happened, she had no idea. The booking in the appointments diary clearly stated 2 p.m. She *couldn't* have got it wrong. It wasn't like her to make such a mistake. It didn't make sense.

'Never mind that,' he snapped. 'Give them my apologies. Make them comfortable. Offer them refreshments. Find the files. Get Clara on the case and get her to see them *A-S-A-P!'* He fired orders at her like bullets.

Kate jumped up from her desk. Clara! Her stomach tightened. Clara had a way of making junior staff feel inferior just by looking at them. She was frightening. She was also French, Kate realised with relief. Her own French was, at best, sketchy.

Keen to redeem herself, she jumped up from her desk and walked briskly across the office floor to Clara's office. Her cheeks burned and her stomach clenched in knots as she quickly explained the situation. Clara glared at her, slowly rose from her desk and smoothed down her already immaculate designer suit in a deliberately controlled way.

'Bring them to my office immediately,' she ordered.

Kate hurried away, eager to amend her error and transform the disaster into a successful meeting. Relieved to find her French was not completely forgotten, she passed on Erik's apologies and led the visitors to Clara's spacious and airy office.

Clara rose from her chair, her right hand extended gracefully in welcome. Once they were all seated, she dismissed Kate's attempt to offer tea and coffee with a glare.

'That will be all, *thank you,' she* snapped, with an icy tone that sent shivers down Kate's spine.

Gratefully, Kate beat a hasty retreat back to the safety and obscurity of her own desk, where she checked and rechecked her daily calendar and the office appointment diary. Both clearly stated 2 p.m. so it didn't make sense that the French representatives had arrived at the wrong time. She didn't make mistakes like that. Couldn't have.

Shaking her head in disbelief, Kate stared at her phone. The appointment was definitely scheduled for 2 p.m. She quickly checked through her emails. Yes, a confirmation that Mr Danielsen would be happy to meet their representatives at 2 p.m. that afternoon. So *how* had this come about? One thing was certain. It was her job to organise appointments and meetings and to ensure they ran smoothly. This was her responsibility and now it was her problem.

She had put everything she had into the Mulberry Park portfolio. It had paid off and been hugely successful. But since taking it, so much had gone wrong. Time and again, little mistakes had eaten away at her confidence, and although nothing could be proven, Kate was sure these blunders and miscommunications were not of her doing. But who would be undermining her like this? And why? Was she being paranoid, thinking this way?

Without concrete evidence, how could she present her case to Erik? All he knew was that recently things did not run smoothly when she was involved. They should do. They really should. She checked and double-checked her figures, dates and appointments. She diligently took her own portfolio work home and studied at weekends and evenings. Something wasn't adding up, not making sense. And what on earth was the matter with Erik lately? He never would have reacted like that over a bungled meeting appointment a few weeks ago. Why was he so on edge? Everyone had noticed he wasn't his usual self. No one seemed to know why.

15

Realisations

Shirley sat back on her heels to admire her work. She had been busy all morning planting little pots of colour in her garden. By early spring they would flourish into a gorgeous rainbow carpet that edged her emerald green lawn and dripped from baskets hanging from the entrance and side of the house. She loved her home and took great joy in her garden, which kept her active and fit.

As she worked, she thought of Lauren with her quiet air of intelligence and steadfast loyalty, but who had been so appallingly abused by her ex-husband in London; Kate who had such energetic optimism and a boundless enthusiasm for life but had been crushed by that charismatic trickster.

What was wrong with these fickle boys that they couldn't recognise a Heaven-sent blessing when it fell into their lives? Neither of them deserved her daughters. If Brian had been here, they would not have gotten off the hook so easily! Quite frankly, she would have happily boxed their ears for them if she had the chance. Might have knocked some sense into their thick heads.

She forcefully plucked at a stray groundsel weed that dared to poke through the paving stones in frustration.

* * *

On Friday afternoon Lauren had just finished cleaning the shop's worktable and tying a delicate silver ribbon around the last of the orders. She had made several early springtime bouquets of tulips, gerberas, chrysanthemums, iris and tiny Alstroemeria lilies, each one an array of glowing colours.

This one would find its way to Kate. Lauren smiled. Julia had gone with Craig on the deliveries this afternoon so she had enjoyed an afternoon of rare peacefulness and was looking forward to seeing her sister later. She still seethed when she thought of how badly Kate had been let down by that bloody scoundrel James. It was a shame she ever met him. She deserved better and Lauren was going to make sure her younger sister knew it.

Standing back to admire her work, her attention turned to the scene unfolding like an afternoon matinee outside the shop window. Out in the high street, some people walked hurriedly as if time itself were running out. Others sauntered along, taking all the time in the world, pausing to gaze into brightly lit shop windows. Young couples walked hand in hand, heads bowed together as if whispering great plans of conspiracy. Older couples strolled side-by-side, an easy companionship keeping them in step with each other.

A familiar nagging feeling demanded Lauren's attention. The notion that she was alone and would likely always be cut deep into her soul; the sense that life was somehow passing her by; that families and happy relationships were wonderful events that happened to other people – but not to her. Maybe it would be good to have someone special in her life. Someone who would share her dreams, plans and ideas. Someone who would look to a hopeful and bright future with her. Someone who would grow old with her.

She allowed herself the luxury of succumbing to the daydream for a few blissful minutes, idly tickling Gretchen behind her ears. For the first time in ages, Lauren felt a hint of loneliness, even regret, for the wasted time spent on her own. She had thought she was fine, going her own way along life's path, until she'd appeased everyone and tried dating. That had failed, and while she had always suspected it would with Erik, it had reminded her what she was missing. To her surprise, she felt a tear trickle through her lashes and heard herself sob. Desperately, she wiped her face with her sleeve and choked back another errant sob. Someone might come into the shop. No one should cry this obviously in public.

The sharp slam of a van door at the back of the shop jolted Lauren back into awareness. Happy chatter and laughter signalled that Julia and Craig had returned from the deliveries.

She forced a smile as they entered the workroom. 'All OK?'

'Yes, fine,' Julia said. 'That's all the deliveries taken care of. Mission accomplished.'

'Great. Now you're here I think I'll go out for a few minutes. Get some fresh air. We could both do with it.'

'Go.' Julia waved her away. 'Enjoy. Take your time. We'll be fine.' Craig nodded in agreement.

'Thanks. I have my phone with me if you need me.'

Lauren clipped Gretchen's lead onto her collar, slipped on her coat, tied a scarf deftly around her neck and left the shop.

How lucky she was to have such wonderful assistants. They were worth their weight in gold. And what a treat to have an outing in the afternoon.

At the park, Lauren threw a tennis ball for Gretchen, who bounded after it gleefully. Afterwards, Lauren bought a coffee from a quaint little café on a corner and chose a peaceful seat surrounded by garden beds. A squirrel jumped from a tree to the paving in front of them, then up into the low branches of a sapling. A young man bent and pointed it out to a child, who laughed and stamped his feet in delight.

Lauren smiled and sipped her coffee. How exciting it must be to show a little one all the new and wonderful things life had to offer, she thought wistfully.

A few obscure figures passed by, striding purposefully along while talking into their phones, hurrying to or from work, their cars or the shops. It seemed as if the world was full of love that mostly went unspoken as people went about their business, hurried and distracted. Deadlines had to be met, jobs had to be attended and chores had to be done... people everywhere working all day for their loved ones, the special ones who loved them and were lucky enough to be loved in return.

A young couple walked either side of a chubby toddler, stooping slightly, each holding one of his hands. Lauren imagined what it would be like to have a family of her own. Her mother's words echoed through her memory as Lauren realised this blissful scene portrayed a life that exceeded her expectations. Could there be anything more wonderful? Anything more worthwhile? To have a family with someone you loved and trusted.

Someone smart. Handsome. *Special.*

Her thoughts drifted to Greg and she caught herself wondering how he was. She hadn't seen him since that day at Alverston Manor. What a wonderful afternoon that had been, filled with awe and surprises. She had enjoyed every minute of being with him, discovering the elegant old manor house, seeing the impressive gardens, meeting Greg's beautiful horses and above all, the wonder of their special Mirage Tree. Momentarily, she was caught up in a blissful recollection of watching the beautiful illusion of light playing on the bark of the silver birch; the white roses, the scent of clear, sweet air – and Greg being so close to her.

Dazed, she came back to the present with a shock of pain like a lightning bolt striking her heart. Greg loved Janelle. He had only been kind to her. A deep well of heartbreaking realisation created a wishful longing inside her so tangible it hurt.

* * *

Lauren couldn't help admiring the view over the moors as she drove towards her sister's apartment. The stunning streaks of colour in the sky above took her breath away for a few seconds; the sunset bathed her world in gorgeous soft light of scarlet and golden hues, striking against intense purple from the wild heather and yellow gorse bushes. There was no doubt about it, Dartmoor in springtime was beautiful. God's own still life painting.

Lauren parked outside the smart apartment block in the dim early evening light, thankful that Kate had thought to leave the outside lights on for her. She pressed Kate's intercom, announced herself and the front door opened.

'Come on up!' Kate sang.

Kate's apartment was on the top floor and as she rode up in the elevator, Lauren realised how much she was looking forward to this evening. The sisters had always been close, but since Lauren had opened the shop and Kate had started working in the city their time together had been limited, life taken over by commitments and obligations. There was so much catching up to do!

'Hi!' Kate's face lit up at the sight of the bouquet. 'These are for *me*? Oh, Laurie, they're simply *gorgeous*!' She buried her face in the flowers before hugging her sister warmly.

Laurie hugged her back, overcome by such a strong sense of connection that it was as if no time had elapsed since they'd last been together. There was no doubt or uneasiness to address, simply a feeling of perfect understanding as they fell into resuming a joyful and relaxed companionship.

We might be sisters - but we are best friends too, Lauren realised.

'Tell me everything,' she urged as Kate rummaged through the stark white cupboards of her show-home kitchen, gathering coffee mugs, teaspoons and a china vase for the flowers.

The kettle boiled and the sisters were soon settled for the evening. A look of pained concentration crossed Kate's pretty features.

'Oh, Laurie.' She turned her mug slowly in her hands. 'I feel so *foolish*. I mean, how could I possibly not have realised James was seeing someone else? I knew there was something wrong, I just didn't know what I could do to put it right. I thought it was something I had said or done. Then…seeing them together like that. It was such a shock.'

Kate looked exhausted. She had no doubt replayed this scene in her mind a thousand times. Lauren reached for her hand, feeling her sister's pain as acutely as if it were her own, but said nothing. Kate needed to talk.

'I trusted him, Laurie. I thought everything would work out OK. I was so happy when we got together, everything was perfect, but then it went so badly wrong. I just feel so gullible. So... so... *stupid!*' Kate's face crumpled.

Lauren suddenly realised she hadn't talked to anyone else about this. How could she? It involved two of her colleagues, people she had to see and deal with at work. That had to be incredibly tough.

She pushed her coffee aside and enveloped her a protective embrace, letting her sob quietly. It reminded her of thunderstorms when they were children. She had reassured Kate then as she was doing now.

Poor Kate. She was too delicate to bear all this grief. Lauren shifted slightly as Kate slumped against her shoulder, overwhelmed by exhaustion and grief. For a few minutes Lauren simply held Kate, letting comfort and healing flow to her sister and dearest friend.

Then she spoke gently but firmly. 'Now listen to me. You are *not* at fault here. None of this came about because of anything you did, or didn't do. There was nothing you *could* do. You just had the misfortune to be duped by selfish, worthless people. You are *NOT* foolish or stupid. You are beautiful, smart and kind, and if James can't see that, he's more stupid than the day he was born. More fool him for losing the best thing that has ever happened to him.'

Lauren released her hold and brushed Kate's hair back from her forehead. She pulled a bunch of clean tissues from the depths of her purse and pressed them into her sister's hands. Kate dabbed at her eyes.

'There now.' Lauren smiled approvingly. 'You'll be fine, better off without him. And you'll come back – the shining star you always have been, but brighter and more beautiful!' She squeezed Kate's hand and received a weak smile in return. 'Just remember what you always tell me – what goes around comes around. Karma will have its way – you always believed that, didn't you?'

'Thanks, Laurie. Yes, I suppose I do believe that. I've certainly learned a lesson or two. I won't ever be so trusting again!'

'Give it time, Katie. You'll find someone much kinder, you'll see. Someone far more worthy of you, and honest. You'll see that I'm right.'

'I don't know. I think I'll just concentrate on work and being independent for a while. Safer that way! Anyway, enough of my problems. How about you and Erik? Is everything going OK?'

'Uh…not exactly.' Lauren gave a rueful smile.

'Oh, Laurie!' Kate cried in dismay. 'I had a feeling *something* had happened, Erik seemed so uptight last week, but I didn't like to ask what was wrong. I was sure you two would be absolutely fine together. Whatever can have happened?'

'Nothing bad or dramatic,' Lauren began, and then grinned as she remembered Erik wrestling Buddy that fateful evening. 'Well, not *too* dramatic,' she added, and explained the whole scenario.

Kate stared at her incredulously. 'Oh. My. *God!* That's got to be the funniest thing I've heard in *weeks!*'

'You should have been there,' grinned Lauren. 'There was poor Erik, the epitome of valour, bravely fighting off that monster dog armed only with a bedraggled bouquet.'

The pair dissolved into helpless laughter.

'I wish I had been,' Kate gasped at last. She dabbed away the tears of laughter and shook her head. 'My immaculate, razor-sharp, awesome boss defending my sister with a bunch of flowers.' The thought set her off again and she fought to regain her composure. 'Erik would certainly be gallant enough, it's exactly the sort of reaction he *would* have. Pure courage.'

'I know!' Lauren laughed. 'Poor Erik. No wonder we've broken up. He probably thinks we're all crazy in the countryside.'

'Aw, no - he wouldn't think that. But seriously, Laurie – you are OK about it? Not too upset?'

'Well, I was a little disappointed, of course.' Lauren smiled wistfully. 'He was lovely. Really he was. I couldn't fault him – he was very kind and attentive. But… I don't know. I just couldn't appreciate the way he lived. Too many differences, there was always so much happening for him. He couldn't have got along with Gretchen and I was just not comfortable in the limelight. You know I prefer rural life to the city. I'm a country girl at heart. I guess we just had different expectations of life. I only hope I haven't upset him too badly, he doesn't deserve it.'

'I am sorry.' It was Kate's turn to hold her sister's hand.

'Ah! It's fine. Really it is. All water under the bridge now. We were like chalk and cheese from the start.' Lauren shrugged. 'I think it's always best to be honest about these things. Besides, I have a feeling I'm destined to be on my own now. I have everything I need. The shop keeps me busy and I love it. It takes a lot of my time and there's always something to do there. I doubt I'll find anyone special – I don't have the time!' She couldn't help a slight twinge of regret.

'Aw, Laurie!' Kate protested. 'You don't know that. Someone special will come along for you.'

'I don't know,' Lauren murmured doubtfully, half to herself. 'Perhaps it's just not meant to be for me. I mean, I have my business, my home, Gretchen, and *you*!' She pulled a comical face and made Kate smile. 'I'm too busy, really I am.'

'It seems as if there's a shortage of nice, trustworthy single guys to date,' Kate lamented. 'They must be out there somewhere, I'm sure of it. Other people seem so happy together. I just don't know why not me.' Kate stared wistfully at the mug cradled in her hands. 'It's here, it's wonderful and special – then *whoosh!* It's gone! Like... it's like love is just an *illusion.*'

Greg slipped involuntarily into Lauren's mind.

'Or they're taken already. It's as if love is out there all around us all the time. But when you look for it, it fades and disappears.'

She thought of Erik, and the rapidly changing, fashionably cosmopolitan life he led. 'No certainty. No promises.'

Then, with a deep chasm of regret that threatened to choke her, Lauren's thoughts turned to her failed marriage and Mike who had left her. 'It's not what you thought it was. Not real.'

Like a mirage, she thought, sadly. *You think it's there but it isn't.*

'I think we need a change of subject,' she said. 'How are things at Clarence and Fulton?'

Kate tucked her feet beneath her on the sofa. 'That's the thing, Laurie. Everything was going so well. I was proud of my Mulberry Park success and Erik was so pleased with the outcome we all went out for drinks to celebrate. Thankfully,

James and Cynthia stayed away.' She tossed her head defiantly. 'Not that I'd have cared if they hadn't. I wasn't going to let them spoil my evening.'

'Good for you.' Lauren grinned. 'That's the spirit.'

Kate frowned and twisted a loose thread in the sofa fabric. 'The only trouble is, ever since that night things haven't been going smoothly. Missing files, bungled appointments, that sort of thing. Mistakes I don't usually make, and I can't work out why.'

'Hmm. Have you spoken to Erik about it?' Lauren asked.

'No. He's busy enough and, well, I wouldn't want to bother him with it. Besides, I wouldn't know what to say. In his eyes I must look completely incompetent, but that's not me and I can't work out what's going on.'

'I hope my breaking up with him hasn't caused you any problems.'

'No, of course not. Erik wouldn't treat me badly because you'd stopped going out with him. Honestly, he's far too professional and focused for any such pettiness. But he did mention he's going away for a couple of months on sabbatical soon. I guess he needs a break. But as for the other stuff that's been going on, I simply don't understand what's happening.'

Sounds suspicious, Lauren thought. Not like the meticulous Kate she knew, with her perfectionist approach and eye for detail.

'Well, maybe just run it past him next week before he leaves,' Lauren advised. 'I'm sure he'll understand.'

'Maybe.' Kate sounded doubtful. 'Anyway, it might just have been a run of bad luck and everything will be back on track.'

'What if it isn't?' said Lauren. 'Promise you'll speak to

Erik about these mysterious problems. Remember what Grandpa used to say: 'There's no time like the present. Time and tide wait for no man!'

16

Discovery

The start of a new week. Kate wearily rubbed her eyes as she waited for the computer screen to light up. She was the first into the office this morning, determined to get ahead and make a good impression this week; but she had slept poorly. Anxiety and upset had crept into her mind in the small hours and kept her awake. As her screen flickered into life, she decided to check her horoscope for the day.

Virgo: All is not lost, on this tide of change, despite recent setbacks and secrets hidden from plain view. Smash open that bottle and find the message for you inside! This is the time for new love and luck, your ship will soon come in; but can you make the one who is riding the highest waves see things from your point of view?

Surely this was the week her luck would turn around – sooner or later something had to change for the better.

Kate sipped her coffee and idly flicked though her emails, disregarding the unimportant ones and those she had already read. One in particular caught her eye, from Brooke and Co, the clients she had lost the week before. Running her fingers though her hair she read and reread the email. It didn't make sense.

Further to the report you submitted our clients have on this occasion decided to decline your offer-

Hold on a minute. *What* report? She hadn't written or submitted a report to them. The email had also been sent to her line manager, general manager, Cynthia and Erik. Wait! Why Cynthia? Strange… she hadn't realised Cynthia was part of the Brooke and Co. team.

Oddly, ever since that woman had joined the office a month ago, things had started going wrong. Coincidence? Probably, she told herself, and shrugged off any thoughts of suspicion.

Flicking through her memos, she noted Cynthia's name had cropped up on a few of Kate's projects and she had been copied into several emails. Including, most notably, one from the French clients who Clara had seen at short notice. Strange again.

Kate made a mental note to ask Erik's personal assistant if she was aware of Cynthia being included in her team. Had they advised Kate of this? No. She was certain she would have remembered an email or verbal instruction that they were to work together. There had been no such order. Had the update been inadvertently overlooked? That didn't sound right either. There must be a simple explanation. Whatever it was, she was determined to get to the bottom of it.

11 a.m. Coffee break time. Thankfully, Kate stood up from behind the computer and made her way to the vending machine. On her way past a few colleagues she stopped briefly and shared a few words. As she passed Cynthia's desk an open drawer containing a blue folder caught her eye.

Kate froze, her blood suddenly turning to ice in her veins. It couldn't be... could it? Her missing work? Steadily, aware she was being watched, she forced herself to continue walking to the machine as if nothing was wrong. She would investigate further, but now was not the right time.

At lunchtime, Kate followed Maria to the staff canteen. She collected her tray and made a beeline for Maria's table before anyone else could join her.

'Hi, mind if I join you?'

'Not at all.' Maria smiled good-naturedly.

'I wanted to ask if you knew the French clients' appointment time had been changed. I must have missed the communication if that was the case.' Kate forced herself to speak steadily and remain calm.

'Hmm, yes, there *was* something odd about that,' Maria said. 'The time was moved from 2 p.m. as I remember, because you'd requested an earlier appointment. Cynthia came to my office to let me know—'

'Oh, *did* she?' Kate was unable to keep her indignation to herself. 'Well, I certainly *did not* ask her to move the appointment time and I had not realised we were working together on that particular portfolio.'

'Yes. I thought it was strange she would request it instead of you, but you were so busy with the Mulberry Park portfolio I didn't get a chance to run it past you. I thought she was doing you a favour by running an errand for you.' Maria frowned. 'Perhaps there's been some miscommunication? A misunderstanding, perhaps?'

'Yes,' Kate agreed, trying to keep the anger out of her voice. 'I think *perhaps* there has.'

* * *

'Thank you, everybody, that's it for today,' Erik called from his office. 'Thanks for a great job well done!'

'I'll stay behind an hour or so,' Kate called, more cheerfully than she felt. 'I have a few things to finish up.'

When the office doors had closed behind the last person and the bright lights in the corridor had flickered off, Kate made her way to Cynthia's desk. Her heart thumped in her chest as she opened the drawer. Yes, those were her files all right.

Containing *her* work. *Her* time. *Her* effort.

Closing the drawer carefully to prevent disturbing the contents, she returned to her own desk and wrote a simple and direct email to Erik, requesting a private meeting with him at his earliest convenience.

* * *

The next morning, to her disappointment, Erik was not at the office. He had gone to Paris to meet some important new clients and wasn't due to return until Monday. He hadn't replied to her email. Instead, she was surprised to receive an official letter from Clara, his second in command, asking to see her at 10 a.m. sharp in her office. What was this about? Could she access Erik's emails? Kate doubted it. More likely, Cynthia had put Clara up to this. Kate was sure Cynthia had seen her recognise the blue files in her desk drawer yesterday.

Warily, Kate took a deep breath. She had an increasing sense of foreboding about this meeting, and wished with all her being that Erik was here. She would have been a lot more confident of being heard fairly.

Clara looked up disdainfully from her MacBook screen as

Kate entered her office.

'Kate, I want you to know we are extremely grateful for all the effort you have given Clarence and Fulton to date. The way you handled the Mulberry Park portfolio was excellent with unexpectedly superb outcomes. You've always been an asset to us, a very valuable member of our team.'

Kate felt her stress escalating and her nerves teetered on edge at the tone of Clara's insincerity. Her fists clenched involuntarily with tension. What was she doing here? What was this about? Why was her success unexpected? She was bloody sure of one thing; Clara didn't mean a single word about her being a valuable asset. Kate was convinced that the only person valuable to Clara Beaufort was Clara Beaufort herself.

'However…' Clara paused, presumably for effect, a look of fake concern upon her face. 'Recently there have been some issues… *mistakes.*' She paused again to emphasise the implications and let her meaning sink in.

Kate's nails dug into her palms. She was acutely aware that she was in the firing line here. Whatever lies were being concocted behind her back, Clara was going to make sure Kate carried the blame.

'Perhaps the stress of this position has been too much for you?' Clara arched a perfectly shaped eyebrow. 'We care about your wellbeing at work and we decided you might benefit from a break. You could take a new, easier position in a less challenging environment. I'm happy to inform you there is such a position for you at our suburban office in Crownhill.'

Kate's cheeks burnt with indignation. This wasn't a request she realised, as she swallowed the lump in her throat. Clara was inferring that she and Erik were in agreement - but he wasn't even here to speak to her directly. It was clear Clara had absolutely no concern whatsoever for 'her wellbeing' and she couldn't trust Clara to be speaking the truth, but standing up to her without support from a senior colleague wasn't going to be easy. Heated indignation surged through Kate. This wasn't fair! None of this was her doing! The mistakes weren't even her fault!

She took a deep breath. 'I realise there have been a few problems.' Kate spoke deliberately, trying to keep the upset from her voice. 'I have discovered some detrimental information regarding recent events.'

Clara rounded on her with a glare that would instantly turn water to ice. *'What do you mean?'*

Her words, piercingly sharp like a serrated knife, carved into Kate's soul. She summoned all her courage and forced herself to sit upright and steadily meet Clara's icy stare and defend herself as calmly as possible. 'Regrettably, it seems there have been hidden problems out of my control that have caused these issues to occur.'

At that moment, she was thankful she was sitting down, as she doubted her legs would support her. 'I found an email to Brooke and Co. that I hadn't written and subsequently noticed Cynthia had been communicating with them without my knowledge. There have been other...'

'If this is an attempt to excuse poor work ethic then I am afraid it is not working for me,' Clara interrupted, with dangerous impatience.

Kate leaned forward, indignation rising inside her. 'No, Clara, listen to me please. I really am trying to explain—'

'You *cannot* blame another member of the team for your shortcomings!' Clara fired at her. 'You are lucky we decided to give you another chance and you are to be transferred to the suburban office. Report there at 9 a.m. Monday morning. I wish you well with your new position. Thank you. That is *all*. You may go.'

Indignation gave way to frustrated anger and Kate opened her mouth to protest, but promptly closed it again. To pursue the issue with Clara was pointless. Better to bide her time and speak to Erik when he returned.

Whenever that might be.

* * *

On Monday morning Kate defied Clara's order to report to the suburban branch and instead arrived an hour early at the office. Erik still had not responded to her request for a private meeting but he was due back and she had to take a chance that he would hear her side of the story.

At 8 a.m. sharp she knocked briskly on his office door and waited hesitantly.

'Come!' his clear voice rang out.

The minute she opened the door her heart sank and she felt overwhelmed with apprehension. Clara was with him, her chair moved closely next to his and leaning towards him. Her scowl left Kate with no doubt she had interrupted a private conversation. No doubt Erik had been thoroughly briefed on the previous week's events.

Erik looked up in surprise. 'Kate, I thought you were to report to the other office today?'

'I wanted to speak with you first. Please may I have a moment of your time?'

'Yes, of course.'

He exchanged a few brief words with Clara about the day's

agenda and she left, glaring at Kate in passing.

'What can I do for you?' Erik asked.

This was her chance to explain to a manager she trusted. Kate sat opposite him and clasped her hands in her lap to stop them shaking, pleased she had rehearsed the points in her mind all weekend.

His frown deepened as she explained about the mysterious emails from Cynthia to Brooke and Co., the missing files sighted in Cynthia's desk drawer, and Maria's confirmation that it was Cynthia's request to move the French clients' meeting to 11 a.m.

'I hate to say it but I believe she has been sabotaging me.'

'This is a serious accusation.' Erik spoke slowly and folded his hand on his desk. Then he leaned back in his chair. 'Are you one hundred percent sure?'

'Yes, I am sure. I know this is serious, and I wouldn't speak up unless I was certain. I have the original data on my computer. I can prove it is my work. Erik—' she looked directly into his eyes. 'I am so sorry about this. I don't want any trouble.'

She was aware of her fingernails digging into the palms of her hands, her breathing fast and sharp. Her throat tightened. 'Please, just ask Maria about the appointment time change. She can confirm what I have said.'

Erik sat for a moment, studying her thoughtfully. Then he slowly rose from his desk and, with great deliberation, strode into Maria's office and closed the door. Minutes later, which seemed like an eternity to Kate, the door burst open.

'Come with me' he ordered, his mouth set in a grim line. 'I don't have time for games.'

Kate meekly followed him and all eyes were upon them as

he marched up to Cynthia's desk.

'Cynthia, would you mind telling me what's in your desk drawer?' he asked quietly. Her look of surprise changed to realisation when she saw Kate standing just behind Erik, nervously chewing her lip.

'Why? Nothing that shouldn't be,' she declared.

'I'll ask you again: what do you have in your desk drawer?'

'Nothing,' mumbled Cynthia, glancing around her nervously before bowing her head.

'Open the drawer!' he demanded.

Cynthia did not move a muscle.

'Open it – *NOW!*' he boomed.

Cynthia flinched visibly, face flushed red. Reluctantly she obeyed.

'Hand me those files.' Erik's face looked like thunder. He turned to Kate. 'These are yours?' She nodded silently in reply.

'I'll need you to bring me your original data as soon as possible. Come and see me tomorrow morning at 9 a.m. sharp. Cynthia, I'll make an appointment in Personnel for you to attend. That's it. Everyone back to work!'

* * *

Back at his office, Erik pushed 'send' on the emails he had just written. It was time for a few changes around here.

The first was a recommendation for a senior to fill an opening in Clarence and Fulton's smart office in Paris. Clara would be perfect for that position. They could send her the information and she could think it over. It was a generous relocation package, good salary, apartment and car included.

He hoped she'd take it. It had been a long time since they

had seen eye to eye on how to run the business and, frankly, she was becoming impossible to have around. He was tired of ignoring her constant flirtation and suggestiveness. Didn't the bloody woman ever take no for an answer? It was becoming embarrassingly obvious to the staff and even some of the clients, and her behaviour had even impacted on his brief relationship with Lauren. He was still angry about that. Thankfully, next week she would be out of his hair; she was attending an all-expenses-paid business conference in Bath for four days, which Erik knew was just an excuse to have a break in a luxury spa hotel. It would give him time to sort a few issues out around here before he went on leave.

Erik sat back in his chair and ran his fingers through his hair and took a deep breath. His decision to have a break was probably long overdue. He had been away many times on short business trips abroad but this time he had allowed himself the luxury of three months to go home to Norway. He was looking forward to it, a chance to catch the snowboarding championships, have fun, relax and catch up with family and friends.

If he left Clara in charge, goodness knows what mess he would come back to. That would have implications for everyone in the office. With luck, she'd accept the Paris transfer package.

With a sigh, he could not shake the deep-seated feeling of uneasiness about his next email. Sending it left him with the distinct impression he had successfully shot himself in the arm, but even with Clara sorted, there were still underlying problems to address. He had decided to transfer Kate to the Crownhill office *with immediate effect*. He had included an excellent reference – he rarely had the opportunity to write such glowing words. Kate may not really wish to go and he hated coercing anyone into a decision like this, but he was certain it would be for the best.

Leaning back in his luxury leather swivel chair, Erik massaged the back of his neck and shoulders. Stress always made his shoulders ache with tension. Kate might be determined, and she had earned his respect, but she was one of the youngest members of his team and he felt protective towards her. A fresh environment while he was away would do her good. Aside from the sabotage at work, James Mitchell had treated her badly. Erik had never really liked James, had always been wary of his ethics and dodgy business acumen. The man was capable of stooping pretty low to clinch deals at times and his brow furrowed at the recollection of recent events. A good team relied on communicating and working well together, and recently that was not happening. He took a sip of water, deep in thought. Decisions had to be made – and fast. Clara obviously had some issue with poor Kate and she and Cynthia had behaved abominably towards her. This whole situation had raised the issue of office bullying and he intended to treat that as a priority. It started today, with moving Kate to safety. She was far too valuable an asset to be destroyed by the office cats.

Transferring Kate would also be a good move for the Crownhill team, who had been struggling to meet their quotas for months. Their end of financial year statistics had been nothing short of abysmal. If Kate worked half as well there as she had here, Erik had no doubt they would soon be hitting their marks. Exceeding them, even. Lastly, this plan would be best for him, Erik thought, with an element of regret. He liked Kate. *Really* liked her. She had great potential and her integrity and ingenuity was like a breath of fresh air in the office. He would miss her enthusiastic, vibrant energy around the place.

It had been a few weeks since he and Lauren had parted company. He had been sorry of course, but they had only dated a few times and parted amicably enough, both agreeing there were insurmountable differences between them. He had been determined not to let his break up with Lauren affect his relationship with Kate or his work in the office. He'd have to make sure Kate understood that.

17

The Conference

Great.

Clara triumphantly zipped up her bulging vanity case. 'That's everything. Four days away in an all-expenses-paid luxury hotel. Suits me *just fine.'*

Work had been such a tiresome travesty lately. Erik had been preoccupied with Miss Demure but Dumpy, and Cynthia had been clingy and whiny. She felt angry with Erik, he had been a fool to turn her down. His constant rejections had deeply upset and offended her, although she'd never let it show. She was *far* better than that fat girl he had been seeing, though she had a feeling something had happened there. He'd been like a bear with a sore head lately. Well, he'd had his chance with Clara Beaufort. If he regretted it now, too bad! He'd have to live with it.

Another thing - what on earth was going on with Cynthia these days? Heaven knew she'd tried to help that girl. Befriended her and backed her up. It certainly wasn't her fault if Cynthia was stupidly going to destroy all her chances.

She'd had it with those losers. They were beyond ridiculous. She needed to get away and she had been looking forward to this conference for weeks. She'd hidden the information from the others in the tram and applied as soon as it was advertised. This was *her* place, no one else's. She was tired of sorting out their stuff ups and problems. They could all damn well get on with it without her.

She was off to a luxury spa hotel in fashionable Bath. A few boring lectures then she'd be free to do whatever she liked – shopping, beauty treatments and – who knew? Maybe a rich, handsome diversion.

Clara smiled to herself. Yes, it was high time she had some fun. This would be a chance to let her hair down. She'd carried them all in that bloody office for far too long.

She damn well *deserved* this break.

* * *

As her taxi neared the hotel, she glanced at her phone. Email from Erik. She sighed impatiently. What did he want now? Whatever it was, he would have to wait. She'd not be contacting work for a few days. It wouldn't make any difference; there would be nothing she could do at the office until next week anyway. Nothing was going to spoil this trip for her, least of all that self-centred fool, Erik Danielsen.

Her taxi pulled up outside the hotel front, busy with guests coming and going. Leaving her Louis Vuitton luggage with the valet, she went straight to reception to collect her key. Annoyingly, there were a few people in front of her. She folded her arms and glared at the women in front of her. She'd have to join the queue.

Suddenly a familiar face caught her attention. She whipped

around in his direction to get a better look. It couldn't be. Surely not! James Mitchell from the office. Honestly, couldn't she ever get away from the bloody place?

Although, he wasn't bad looking. Pretty fit, too. Nice body under that designer suit, she'd bet. Interesting, though. She hadn't realised he would be here.

After checking into her room and unpacking (which largely consisted of throwing her clothes onto a chair and checking out the mini bar), Clara decided to spend the remainder of the day in town. No sense in wasting time. She had several spas and boutique shops on her 'must do' list. She idly flicked through her phone and found a text message from James. He was going to Bath for the week and could she arrange to meet his clients in his absence? *No*, she messaged back. *That is not possible.*

Almost immediately he fired back *Why?*

She smiled at the indignant attitude. Idiot. She wasn't there to do his bidding. But he *might* be useful.

She sent a text back, informing him she already knew he was in Bath, and added his room number.

The reply came straight back. *When did you arrive?*

Clever! She flattered him. He'd obviously worked out she had spotted him checking in. James *could* be smart – when it suited him.

They arranged to have dinner at the hotel later then go out and explore the local nightlife together.

At seven-fifteen Clara met him at the bar. They had agreed on seven, but it didn't hurt to keep a man waiting. Besides, she knew she was worth waiting for. Polished and scented from her glossy hair to the tips of her manicured fingers and toes, and clad in a designer mini dress that showed off her perfectly tanned legs, she knew she looked hot.

Poor James didn't stand a chance.

* * *

'My God!' The exclamation of approval shot into his mind, though luckily he didn't say it aloud. Looking her up and down appreciatively, James felt his ego inflate to fill the room, like a massive soap bubble being blown from a little plastic hoop. She was a vision of wonder all right! He had to stop himself from openly staring in awe at her ample cleavage, tightly clad in smooth black satin. She looked fabulous.

He'd definitely lucked out tonight. Good job he'd managed to stop Cynthia from getting permission to come, for all her whining and moaning. He'd told her it would be boring, and he'd be far too busy to socialise or entertain her so she wouldn't enjoy it. Hell, he'd even had to promise he'd be thinking of her every day. He was glad he'd managed to get away from her for a few days. It was much better to come to these things alone. You never knew what opportunities would come along.

After dinner, Clara suggested going to a new nightclub in town. James didn't much care for the idea. He'd much rather have forgotten the club altogether and skipped to the 'coffee' in his suite, but Clara definitely knew where she wanted to go and what she wanted to do. Apparently, this place was pretty exclusive; a few celebrities had been known to hang out there. Anyway, he didn't have much choice in the matter; if he wanted Clara, this was the price he'd have to pay. One evening at a nightclub was OK, he supposed. He could manage that.

* * *

Their cab pulled up at the kerbside at the club entrance. A

queue of people snaked along the wall and around a corner, far away from them and out of sight. James inwardly groaned. If she thought he was going to join that mob, she had another think coming.

'Look, are you sure this is a good idea? I'm not joining that lot!'

'Don't be silly. Of course not!' She laughed incredulously. The very idea! He could be such a dolt. 'Just follow me.'

Clara picked out the tallest, most prominent doorman who was barking orders into the microphone of his headset. He clearly considered himself to be the leader of the gang. Taking a deep breath in, she pushed her chest out and rolled her shoulders back. She confidently sidled up to him, smiling sweetly, then stood closer than necessary and whispered something in his ear.

Poor bastard doesn't stand a chance! James smirked inwardly. Best just to stand back and let Clara do her thing.

The doorman puffed up, obviously flattered to be paid such attention. He nodded briefly to his mate and the velvet rope opened to let the two of them enter, to the groans of the impatiently waiting hoards behind them.

James slipped his arm around Clara triumphantly. The doorman could look. They all could. Let them. But this amazing beauty was with *him*!

At that moment the blinding white flash of a camera illuminated them in a pool of light. The two of them instinctively looked up towards the flash. Clara gave the cameraman one of her most dazzling smiles and was instantly rewarded with several more flashes. James inwardly shrugged. Must have mistaken them for celebrities. Now to enjoy himself.

* * *

It was 3 a.m. when they left the club, and James was silently fuming. That place had cost him a bloody fortune and Clara had spent most of the night drinking champagne he had paid for and 'networking' with people he hadn't even been introduced to. She'd been far too interested in meeting and greeting influential, wealthy and handsome executives.

It was bloody late too. At least they were heading back to the hotel. Perhaps *now* he'd get what he wanted.

At reception, they collected their respective keys and headed to the elevator together. James had a suite on the third floor, Clara's was (of course) upgraded to the penthouse deluxe suite. As the doors opened on the third floor, James turned to her and smirked, confident she would come with him. After all, he'd treated her well. Paid for everything and agreed to everything she had wanted to do.

Now it was *his* turn to be treated well.

'Night-night!' Clara warbled, drunkenly planting a kiss on his cheek. 'S'you in the morning!'

'It *is* bloody well morning!' he roared. Then, in a softer tone, 'Come back to mine, babe. There's still time, we can party on.'

'Aw, I'm *sooo* tired, sweetie!' Clara simpered, giving him her most angelic smile. 'It's *so* late now. Besides, we still have two whole days. But I had the *best* time! Maybe tomorrow. Patience is a virtue!'

She gave him a playful light shove out of the elevator and blew him a kiss as the doors closed, leaving him standing on the third floor by himself.

* * *

Lauren and Julia were working on a large bridal order. Usually, Lauren would confidently leave Julia to this kind of job, but she had been working slowly the past few days and seemed distracted, slightly upset even. Not wanting to pry, Lauren had simply offered to give her a hand if she needed it today, and Julia had gratefully accepted her help.

'That's beautiful!' Lauren exclaimed, smiling warmly at her young assistant. 'You have such a flair for colours, Julia. You should be proud of yourself!'

Lauren set the beautiful bouquet aside, and prepared to make a start on the smaller posies for the bridesmaid and church aisle decorations.

'Julia,' she began carefully, 'is there something going on? You don't seem quite yourself.'

Julia sighed and put down the piece of ribbon she had been trimming. 'I'm pregnant!'

'That's great – isn't it?'

'It is.' Julia smiled weakly, twisting the ribbon around her hand. 'I mean, it's a surprise, we didn't expect this so quickly, but it's Craig. He thinks we should get rid of Buddy!' Julia's lip trembled. 'He's just so big and strong now. Craig's worried that he'll be too boisterous with the baby. What happens if we have to buy a smaller place of our own? Craig says I won't be able to manage him on my own with a baby too, but honestly, we can't just give him up. We just *can't!* He was to be part of our family!'

'Well, perhaps Craig is right. He *was* a bit of a handful at the puppy school.'

'It wasn't his fault. He was just excited and he wanted to say hello to everyone.'

'Yeah, he was just being friendly.' Craig popped his head

around the workshop door, back from his deliveries. 'Poor Buddy had to spend the entire class in a doggy prison. He didn't deserve that.' He came in and put his arm around Julia. 'All I'm saying is that we probably can't give him the home and attention he needs.'

'I know what you're saying, Craig. Sometimes you have to put their needs ahead of your own and a dog like Buddy shouldn't be cooped up and imprisoned all his life. He needs some countryside to run, and maybe a job to do,' agreed Lauren.

'Yes, but where?' Julia wailed. 'Our parents say they are too old to take on another dog now and our friends are all working and saving for families of their own. No one has time for poor Buddy!' She looked as if she might cry.

'Look, leave it with me,' Lauren said. 'I can't promise, but I will see what I can do. We'll sort something out for him if we can. He needs someone who has a country lifestyle, someone local who knows the countryside and the people in it really well. Someone professional, maybe...someone smart and kind, someone dedicated to animal welfare and ownership.'

Now, whoever could *that* be? Lauren smiled knowingly to herself.

* * *

Later that evening after their walk, Lauren made herself a warm drink and she and Gretchen settled peacefully in front of the fire. As she reached to place her mug on the coffee table and pick up the TV remote control, her eye fell on the card Greg had left her. Thoughtfully, she picked up her phone.

'Alverston Veterinary Practice,' a soft voice with a distinctive French lilt sang down the phone. 'How may we help you?'

Janelle, Lauren realised with a twinge of disappointment. She liked Janelle and was incredibly grateful to her for helping Gretchen, of course; but it would have been nice to speak to Greg again. At the thought of him, Lauren's pulse quickened. For the thousandth time, she thought how lucky Janelle was.

'Hello, Janelle, how are you? Lauren Sinclair here, Gretchen's mum. I hope you don't mind my calling you at home. I have a request.'

'Not at all. Ask away.'

Lauren explained. 'My friends rescued a friendly but over-excitable mastiff puppy and they love him, but he's outgrown their small place and with a baby on the way they really need to find him a safe new home. I'm sure they would like to visit him from time to time.'

'I see. I will speak to Greg when he comes home, yes? I am not sure if we know anyone who can help your friends, but we will give it some thought. One of us will get back to you.'

Lauren thanked her and went back to her coffee and TV. She hoped it would be Greg who got in touch. It would be lovely to hear his voice again. There was something special about the man and the thought of him made her feel blissfully happy and warm inside – though she had no right to feel that way. No right at all.

18

Betrayal

At 9 a.m. sharp the next morning, Kate had collected her work, ready to present to Erik as he had instructed. Standing outside his office door, still a little shaken from yesterday's proceedings, she summoned up her courage and rapped confidently on the frosted glass door pane.

'Come.' Sharp and clipped. She took a deep breath and opened the door.

'My work, as you requested.' Kate dropped it lightly onto his desk.

'Please take a seat, Kate.' Erik looked up at her kindly. He actually looked pleased to see her, Kate realised with surprise.

'I wanted to tell you how pleased I am with your progress here. You have been an asset to us – to me, actually. Your work ethic has been excellent and you are one of the most promising junior members of our sales team. I am aware you have had some difficulties lately and I am impressed that your work continues to be of a consistently a high standard.'

That was a relief. Kate smiled. At least now she wouldn't

have to go to the quieter office. She would stay here and prove to everybody that she was an invaluable team member.

Erik leaned forward in his chair. 'That's why I am so pleased to be able to offer you a new position at our Crownhill office.'

Wait –What was that? Kate stared at him. Had she heard him correctly? 'Crownhill?'

'Yes, there's a new opportunity opened up for a promotion there. We need a dedicated senior in sales to improve their team and raise standards and I think you would be perfect for it.'

Kate sat in dumb silence. He didn't want her here! She was being moved to the smaller suburban office after all. Clara had won and she was bloody well being pushed to move offices even though none of the recent problems had been her fault! Her distress turned to anger in an instant.

'But Erik, none of the problems we have encountered recently were my fault -'

'I realise that. It's not a decision I am taking lightly.' He smiled kindly at her. 'This is a great opportunity. I think it would suit you very well, Kate.'

He meant it! Could he really believe this was for the best? Kate's mind was a whirl of emotion. Was this because of his split with Lauren? She bit down hard on her lip, forcing herself to be sensible. *No. Erik wouldn't be that petty.* He wasn't sending her away because of any recent personal situation of his, she was sure of that. It would be Clara behind this. But Erik was the boss. He had every right to move her to another office and there was sweet nothing she could do about it. The realisation hit her with the impact of a speeding train.

'I trust this change of scene will meet with your approval,

and you will rise to the challenge,' he said. 'I am sure you'll be superb there. Kate, I want you to know this is not a personal decision for me in anyway, it has nothing to do with the past.'

Was he patronising her now? *Dammit, he'd live to regret this decision!* She was bloody well going to make a star of herself. Kate stood over him and gripped the edge of his desk so hard her knuckles turned white. She'd work like she never had before. He thought her quota was good now, in six months she would make sure it had skyrocketed. Then he'd be sorry he let her go! Just watch me, Erik Danielsen, Kate vowed silently.

'If that's all, then please excuse me,' she said. 'I have work to do.'

Erik looked directly at her with a fleeting expression of bemusement, then nodded briefly in dismissal before he lowered his head over his paper-strewn desk.

* * *

Back in his hotel room in Bath, James slammed the door, not caring how much noise he made, and threw his jacket and tie on the bed.

Dammit. He wasn't used to rejection and frustration kept him wide awake.

Never mind, he soothed himself. It was probably the champagne. Of course she'd be tired. Like she said, there was always tomorrow.

The following day passed in a haze of droning lectures, mundane adverts and demonstration workshops from various representatives.

James and Clara spent a good bit of the morning networking and exchanging business cards. Lunchtime rolled around and the two finally caught up with each other in the dining room.

'Not eating?' James asked.

Clara smiled briefly at him. 'No. Just coffee for me. I need the caffeine. I made a few contacts. How are you going?'

'Yeah, not bad.' James couldn't care less about contacts. The only contact he really wanted was with her, under the sheets.

'Want to skip the afternoon?' he asked hopefully. 'I fancy some fresh air. We could catch a movie, or…' His voice trailed and he smiled suggestively. 'Whatever you fancy.'

'Hmm, maybe later.'

A good-looking young man in an expensive designer suit had caught her eye across the room and she began gathering her papers together to leave. 'Later, OK?' she said. 'I'm looking forward to it!'

Then she was gone in a heartbeat.

* * *

Clara decided to skip the afternoon lectures. She had done enough networking; there wasn't a single interesting person left in the room she hadn't introduced herself to and she was sure she had a good grasp of the new technology for business already. Besides, anything she needed she could get from James later.

A nice cold glass of Chablis and a movie was called for, she decided.

As she was about to leave the hotel, she thought perhaps she should leave James a message. She ought to be polite and let him know her plans, especially if he was going to take her to dinner later. She fancied the new place that had opened a few weeks ago, the trendy celebrity magnet in the centre of town that had rave reviews in Cosmo.

She'd get the receptionist to book one of their best tables for 7 p.m. She had better let him know; a place that exclusive wouldn't keep a table waiting for them for long.

* * *

James yawned for the third time in ten minutes. A stocky, middle-aged bloke in the middle of a PowerPoint presentation droned on. It was too warm in the conference room and he'd just about had enough for one day. And where the bloody hell was Clara? She might have let him know if she was going out. He'd have gone too. He could have had a spa or a pint in a pub while she went shopping. Hell, he'd rather be anywhere than sat here by himself, listening to this drivel all afternoon.

Perhaps he'd go to the pub across the road for a swift one. Or maybe two.

James grabbed his jacket from the back of the chair and left the stuffy conference room as inconspicuously as he could. As he passed the reception desk, the concierge beckoned him.

'I have a message for you, Mr Mitchell.'

James read the hastily scribbled note Clara had left. Some restaurant she'd booked for 7 p.m. Fine. Whatever. He didn't know the place, but it made no difference to him where they ate. He'd meet her later.

* * *

As they entered the restaurant, James raised an eyebrow. This place looked special, with a cool atmosphere, high-beamed ceilings and eclectic decor. The tables were well spaced and gleamed with silver and crystal, and a low hum of chatter and piano music complemented the elegance of the place. It was first class. Exclusive. Clara must have done well to get a booking at such short notice. James was impressed – and he wanted to impress her. Very much so.

A waiter approached and introduced himself as Julian. Clara spoke a few words to him and he smiled and led them to a quiet, elevated table at the back of the restaurant, next to a large window overlooking a garden.

Once they were seated, Julian presented the menus with a flourish then left them to peruse the selection. A few minutes later he was back with silver ice buckets containing bottles of sparkling mineral water and Bollinger.

Blimey, James thought. He hadn't expected all this! Clara must have ordered it already. Might as well enjoy it.

There were no prices on the menu, which worried him a bit, but thankfully he'd had a good lunch at the hotel. He wasn't too hungry.

When Julian returned he ordered a steak, chips, a simple green salad and a beer.

'And for madam?' Julian inquired.

Clara placed her menu in front of her and studied it in an unhurried manner.

'The foie gras and lobster with the special salad.'

The food was excellent and they enjoyed each other's company. Clara relaxed as the bubbles worked their magic and James, initially concerned at the cost, decided not to worry. What the heck, you only live once, he told himself. Besides, they'd probably split the bill. He sat back in his chair and smiled at Clara. There was no doubt about it; she was special. A cut above the rest.

At the end of the evening, Clara announced she was going to the powder room. A few minutes later, Julian came into view. Might as well get the tab, James decided, reaching for his jacket. He glanced at the bill, which was placed in front of him a small leather-bound folder, and felt the blood drain from his face.

No! Impossible. There must be some mistake. He must have read it wrong. James took a closer look and inhaled sharply, shock sinking in. Bloody hell! Could that be right? He could pay a small country's national debt with that figure! Surely, this was someone else's bill.

He was about to beckon Julian to check when Clara returned. He straightened up, feeling uneasy. He didn't want embarrass himself in front of Clara and he didn't want to appear cheap, but if this bill was correct, they should split it.

'Ready?' she sang out. 'Oh good, you got the bill already. I'll get the cab fare then. See you outside.' She flashed him a dazzling smile and James deflated inwardly. With an air of defeat, he made his way to the cashier.

The lights of the city passed in a colourful blur against the darkness of the evening from the window of their cab. James had his arm around Clara and to his delight she snuggled into him.

'Your place or mine?' he asked, nuzzling her neck.

'Yours.'

When they arrived James fumbled with the key to his room, one arm around Clara. Suddenly the door gave way and flung wide open. They almost fell into the dimly lit room.

He kissed her with an uncontrolled urgency, his lips covering hers, his weight eagerly crushing against her. She ignored him at first and kicked off her shoes, but then turned her attention to him, and began to welcome his kisses, surprising him by reciprocating the grinding with a hedonistic urgency that matched his desire. Pushing off his jacket and tossing it on the floor, she ran her hands over his smooth, solid body through his shirt.

'You're keen!' He grinned and reached down to unzip his trousers.

She impatiently pushed his fingers away. 'I'll do it.'

James stepped out of his shoes as the pants and belt fell to the floor. Standing there in his shirt and socks, he felt a pang of uncertainty. She was fully dressed; this wasn't how it was supposed to be. Not fair! He'd soon put that right.

'You know, I *love* this dress,' he murmured, pressing feather-like caresses on her neck, her heady perfume filling his mind with new sensations of heightened desire. 'I'd love it even more on the floor.'

He reached around her back and tugged with impatient clumsiness at the zipper.

'Leave it,' her clear voice commanded. 'I'll do it. It's a Christian Lacroix. Genuine.' She eased out of the expensive dress carefully and let it slide to the floor to join the puddle of clothes.

He stood and stared. She was enough to take any man's breath away.

Strikingly Amazonian, Clara stood before him, clad only in the flimsiest cream lace. He ran his tongue over his lips. She was simply magnificent, all smooth, tanned limbs and the tautness of a Victoria's Secret angel.

She gave a low, throaty chuckle and sauntered languidly over to the bed, giving him plenty of time to fully appreciate her toned body. James felt a new rush of desire. On complete autopilot, unaware his feet were even moving, he followed her to the bed.

She turned to look at him with a triumphant smirk.

'It's your turn.'

He thought she was teasing him until he caught her eye; she was looking directly at him, her expression serious, issuing a challenge. Her gaze pierced straight through him. James caught his breath. She was amazing. Every inch of him wanted her now; and he desperately wanted to win her admiration and respect.

Nothing had ever been more important to him.

'You're going to love this!' he promised. 'I do two-hundred sit ups and bench presses a day.'

Clara smiled sweetly at him.

'Nice,' she said after he hastily stripped off his shirt and socks. She reached out and pulled him to the bed.

Afterwards, they lay in the dark, skin to skin, damp and satisfied.

James's mind drifted sleepily. It had been amazing, some of the best sex he'd ever had. Both as fit as athletes, he'd been determined not to let her down and worked hard. She'd reciprocated by giving every bit as good as she'd got! He smiled to himself. She was just incredible, he thought, and drifted to sleep cocooned in a bubble of rosy contentment.

It was as if the world and all its former anxieties were coated in sweet, molten caramel. James was in love.

Suddenly there was movement on the other side of the bed. Surely she didn't want to go again? That was too much – it was time to sleep.

'Honey, I'm tired. Let's sleep now, OK?' He reached out to put his arm around her. Women liked that after sex. Made them feel secure, or some bollocks.

But she wriggled out of his embrace and got up. His sleepy

mind registered that she was moving around in the darkness. What was she doing?

'What the…what's going on?'

'Sweetie, I simply can't share. I need to be in my own bed to sleep properly. You know how it is, right?'

'Uh. Oh. Right. OK.' A wave of surprise washed over him. This never happened to him. Usually he had to think of some excuse to get away. A woman had never left him straight after sex before. 'Please, just come back to bed, baby.'

'Oh, *babeee*, don't be all cross and spoil things,' she said sweetly. 'We had such a great time. I'll see you in the morning.'

She quickly blew him a kiss and with a click of the door she was gone.

* * *

Early next morning, James awoke to memories of the night before and lay on his back staring at the ceiling. The sugary sweetness had worn off with the cold light of day. What had he done wrong? He'd assumed he and Clara would be an item. They were obviously made for each other. He thought she wanted to be with him. Women usually did. Never before had he been pushed aside.

Standing in front of the bathroom mirror, he began to feel foolish. How could this have happened to him? Where was his life going? What was he doing?

Then a thought popped into his mind that was completely unexpected. Why ever had he left Kate? He jolted in surprise. The memory of her unexpectedly slapped him hard, like a punch from behind.

Sweet Katie, with her pretty smile, beautiful hair that smelled of peaches, and her soft laughter – he missed her. So much it hurt. So much he could cry. She had made him feel so good.

But she was gone and – James swallowed hard on the lump in his throat that threatened to choke him – he only had himself to blame. He'd treated her badly. Like a fool, he'd thrown her away because he thought he could do better but in reality, all he'd got was an empty bed, empty promises – and pockets to match. He reeled in shock as stark realisation sunk in. Clara had used him. She'd completely and utterly used him.

19

Confrontation

Cynthia stared in astonishment at the photograph, still unable to believe her eyes. This was worse than any Monday morning she'd ever experienced. She'd had the most awful start to the day; intuitively she knew it was going to get worse.

Out of breath and damp with sweat from having to power walk part of the journey to work because her train had terminated two stops earlier for maintenance, she felt sticky and uncomfortable. If only she'd got something here at the office to change into – a fresh shirt or something. But she hadn't thought to keep a change of clothes here and there was no time to dash out and buy one, because her meeting at the Personnel department was scheduled for nine o'clock. She dare not be late – that would add fuel to an already blazing fire.

Damn!

At the thought of it she felt cold nerves twist her insides into a knot. She pulled another stick of gum – her third in two minutes – from her bag. She hadn't thought anything could be worse or more humiliating than the impending meeting with likely accusations of theft and plagiarism to try and defend, but now there was something much worse for her to deal with.

Outside the newsagents, sitting proudly on a newsstand for the whole world to see, was the front page of the South West Times. As she'd rushed past, a photograph of someone familiar had caught her eye. She'd stopped dead in her tracks, stunned.

There were Clara and James. Together. Outside some swish nightclub.

Clara looked like a goddess, all flawless perfection. She was looking directly at the camera with her dazzling trademark smile. James had his arm firmly around her.

That was bad enough, but it wasn't the end of the world.

It was a shock, but it was bearable.

It was a blow, but it wasn't soul-destroying.

That wasn't what was tormenting her.

What was devastating, torturing her mind and spirit and twisting her heart until she felt it rupture deep within her, was the look on his face.

James's attention was fixated on Clara as if she were the most wonderful woman in the world. Sheer pride and devotion shone from him. Not once had he ever looked at her that way, she realised with devastating clarity. She could not tear her gaze away from the image.

The crushing realisation she had been betrayed hit her full on. With a sob, Cynthia removed her glasses and reached into her bag for a handful of tissues.

James had lied to her, and all the while she had trusted him, believed every smooth, convincingly compelling word.

She had fallen for a man who had promised her she was his perfect partner. They were an unrivalled love match. An unbeatable alliance. He had talked of a beautiful future, full of luxurious choices, travel and stability. Her dream dissolved with her tears. He had used her. He had said he didn't want to leave her to go to the conference and would be thinking of her every day, and she had believed him. Yet here he was, closely entwined with the office beauty queen, a look of smug adoration plastered all over his face.

She had been so easily fooled. Her naivety felt like a white-hot laser cutting into her soul and she crumpled under the pain. She couldn't breathe. She wrapped her arms around her middle and doubled over. Not once had he ever looked at her like that. Not once had he ever looked at her as if he loved her.

At eight fifty-five she stood outside the door of the Personnel department, her stomach in knots and her mouth dry despite all the gum she'd worked through. She'd bravely washed away her tears, re-applied her makeup and tidied her hair, but she had the depressing feeling nothing she did would make much difference to the outcome. It was all going to be a waste of her time.

Oh well. Best get this bloody farce of a meeting over with.

She rapped on the door with more confidence than she felt. Responding to the curt response, she twisted the door handle and took a deep breath, trying to fend off a growing sense of impending doom. She's lost her boyfriend, but she'd bet that wasn't all she'd lose today.

Cynthia was absolutely certain she was about to be fired.

* * *

Late afternoon sun streamed through Erik's office

window. He was quietly contemplating the mornings' events. Cynthia's meeting in Personnel hadn't been easy but he had supported her the best way he could. Returning from that meeting, Maria had asked to see him and informed him James had unexpectedly decided to leave, apparently taking a new position in their London office, effective immediately. While Erik wasn't sorry to see him go, it had left him short staffed. With his pending sabbatical, he would have to act quickly and arrange replacement cover. Maria had immediately set about organising interviews and rearranging his schedule, which meant a lot of disruption and chaos. Those things he could handle, but despite this confidence Erik had a sense of foreboding. A tornado was coming. Things were about to get a thousand times worse.

* * *

Clara stared at her email inbox in disbelief. There had to be some mistake. She'd only been away a few days - less than a week! How could that have possibly been long enough for Erik to have her relocated?

To Paris?

How *dare* he? How dare he have her moved behind her back. She'd been well aware of his lack of interest in her personally, but she'd never had him down as sneaky or underhand. She'd sort out this nonsense. *Right now.* What the hell was he playing at? He could damn well face her and tell her himself if he wanted her transferred.

Clara burst out of her office like an unleashed tigress, ignoring all the startled gapes as she swept across the floor. Without hesitation, not bothering to knock, she threw Erik's door open and slammed it shut behind her.

'What the *bloody hell* do you think you're playing at?' she screamed, looming over his desk.

Erik rose to face her. 'What the devil is going on?'

'I've been away for *five bloody minutes* and I come back to find you've approved a *relocation* for me. What's this about?' Clara couldn't keep the tremor from her escalating voice. 'Couldn't wait for me to go, could you! So you could sort this out behind my back! Just *bloody well* couldn't wait, like the *coward* you are!' Her voice reached a crescendo of anger. 'You didn't have the courage to take me on, be my partner – and now you don't have the guts to face me and tell me about this transfer in person!'

Erik stood frozen, his hands gripping his desk and his face dark with rage. Clara knew she was on dodgy ground but now she had started, the months of pent up frustration and the pain of rejection spewed out; she couldn't stop herself.

'I've been dedicated to you and this bloody office for years. Sorted out *your* ridiculous problems, covered up the s*heer bloody incompetence* of the witless juniors *you* hire, taken *mountains* of work home with me, come in at a *moment's* notice, *backed you up* at *every* turn, *translated endless* documents for the French team. I've shouldered my share of the responsibility for their fuck ups -' She jabbed her thumb over her shoulder at the office floor –'dealt with every kind of fucking mess to save your ass when you weren't here. I am *invaluable here!*' she spat.

'Now, just you listen to me.' Erik's voice was low, controlled and dangerous, like a cobra poised to strike. 'I am tired of your pathetic games. Tired of your twisted attempts at intimidation, your narcissistic, over-inflated, self-driven ego. The only thing you were *ever* dedicated to is your own selfish agenda.'

Erik paused to give her time to take this in, then raised his voice a notch. 'Self-promotion – even at the demise of others – was *always* a career enhancement plan for you. I have watched you influence and manipulate Cynthia with your toxic ploys and I saw how you teamed up with her to bully Kate - and countless others before her. I am exhausted from your unwanted advances, your impropriety and exploitation. I cannot count the number of times you have *seriously* overstepped the mark, despite repeated polite and patient warnings.' He was shouting at her now. 'I cannot count the number of times your sheer unprofessionalism has impacted on my business deals, my reputation – even my *own personal relationship*! Lastly, I am absolutely, one hundred per cent *sick and tired* of covering up your *blatantly serious personal misconduct* to senior management and *giving you chances*! There will be *NO MORE!*' he roared.

Clara sank into a leather swivel chair, speechless, and spun away from him, her face burning with anger, her eyes stinging with tears from the shame of rejection.

Erik turned his back on her and stared out of the window. Neither of them spoke and the silence seemed to stretch interminably.

Then Erik took a deep breath, crossed the floor and opened a cabinet. He poured a measure of cognac into two crystal tumblers and handed one to Clara. She stared at it, then with a slightly trembling hand took it and downed the golden liquid in one gulp. Fire hit the back of her throat with an immediate soothing effect.

She stared at Erik. Had she really been that bad? That obnoxious? She took a deep breath.

'Look, Erik. About us.' Of all the accusations, this was the one that seemed most important to address. 'I didn't mean to cause you any harm. I really didn't set out to upset your ex-girlfriend, whatever her name was. It just seemed obvious we could be *so good* together. I didn't understand why you couldn't see that. We were a good team, weren't were?'

'Yes, we were.' Erik smiled grimly as he swirled the last of his brandy around the bottom of his glass.

To her indignation, Clara found she had to fight hard to keep tears from falling. *Good God, please don't let that happen.* She couldn't cry now. She would rather die! She couldn't live with that humiliation. She bit down hard on her lower lip and tried not to think how genuinely fond of Erik she was. She loved him, she realised. The tears threatened to spill again.

He downed the last of his drink and looked at her levelly. 'We were a *great* team, Clara. Nobody can deny that.' His voice was softer, kinder now, and Clara began to feel a little soothed and humbled by his recognition. 'I will always be grateful for the work you and James have put in here.'

At the mention of James, Clara winced. She hoped she wouldn't have to see him any time soon. He couldn't compare to Erik.

'It's true, our team has achieved *so* much, and I couldn't have done it without you. But I never saw a future for us personally and I made that clear from the start. It's time for some changes and for some of us to move on. That's life – it happens. I am considering my options, too. That's just the way it is. We can't stop progress!' he shrugged. 'Consider yourself lucky to have been offered this transfer. It's a very generous package; apartment, car, relocation expenses. It's a sideways move too, so you will still have a chance to run your own team one day, if you choose to. But – take my advice and learn from this. Learn how to treat people, how to lead and inspire a team. You need to know how to get them on the winning side – *your* side.'

He smiled at her. 'Don't try to control or manipulate others to get what you want. You're smart enough, people will trust you if you are honest and treat them with genuine integrity. I believe you *can* do this, Clara. Think of it as a fresh start.'

Clara took a deep breath, crossed her legs and allowed herself to relax into the depths of the chair. Her eyes brimming with unshed tears, she turned and looked out of the window for a few moments, taking in the sunshine, which played dappled shadows across the rain-slicked glass. A dove took flight, flapping its wings furiously in its effort to rise until it spread its wings and glided on a thermal, soaring high above the rooftops. *Maybe that's me,* Clara thought wryly. *Maybe that dove is me, flapping, fighting, pushing to get up and away and soar.* Maybe this *really is* my chance.

That sounded good. A fresh start. A chance to prove what she already knew in her heart she could achieve, to make it to the top, and build something great for herself in a country she knew and loved. A chance to reconnect with old friends, rebuild relationships with the few family members who knew and loved her. Stop fighting and start living.

'Yes. Maybe I will.' She mused, half to herself. 'Look Erik, I'll grab my coat and bag, and leave now. Please send my other things on to my new address.'

The thought of having to face everyone with a final announcement of goodbye filled her with horror. She wasn't about to put herself through that humiliation.

'Yes, of course. Consider it done. Go home, Clara. Have

a break; take some time to think things through. I'll get the paperwork in place and send it to you. I expect the transfer to go ahead within the month.'

Clara nodded curtly, and stood up. She'd have to collect her things and make for the elevator as briskly as possible. No explanations. Just leave the office and get as far away as she could as quickly as possible. After all, her departure was no one's business but hers.

Now for the hardest part. With her hand resting on the doorknob, she swallowed a lump in her throat and turned to him.

'Erik, just one more thing.'

A frown creased his forehead. Was he perplexed or annoyed? It didn't matter much now.

'Thank you,' she said, and left.

* * *

Cynthia, returning from a late lunch, gave a sigh of relief as she pressed the elevator call button. It had been one of the most harrowing days of her life. The morning personnel meeting seemed to last an eternity. She had been grilled by a senior personnel officer and an executive manager for the best part of two hours about her work ethic, her morals, and the implications of taking a colleague's work without consent to use for her own personal gain. It had been hard work fending off their accusations, and if it hadn't been for Erik's support she would most likely have been fired. He'd explained she had fallen victim to office politics and pointed out that until recently her work record was exemplary. Thanks to him speaking up for her, she'd been given a formal warning and told to take a few hours off, to recover from the ordeal. But she could keep her job.

If she still wanted it.

She taken a long lunch break to recover from the morning's emotional trauma, collect her thoughts and decide what to do. She was expected back at her desk now, but perhaps she'd gather her things and go back home to her parents. It would be a lot easier.

The lift bell signalled its arrival, the door slid open and Cynthia prepared to step in. All comforting thoughts of home immediately vanished as she came face to face with Clara.

'Well if it isn't the office bitch herself!' Cynthia spat, rage boiling up in her.

'*What did you say*?' Clara's voice was icy, as sharp as any gutting knife.

'You heard me, bitch.'

For a few seconds, they glared at each other. Clara raised her hand intending to deliver a resounding slap, then dropped it with a shrug and a sigh as if it wasn't worth the effort.

'Honestly, Cynthia,' she said. 'Let me assure you, he wasn't all that special. Not worth your time or energy, believe me.' For a second her eyes reflected a glimmer of empathy. She pushed past Cynthia, smartly pivoted on her flawless heels and clicked steadily away down the corridor, not missing a single beat.

'Who the *hell* do you think you are? Come back here. Come back this *instant!*' Cynthia screeched in vain at her retreating back.

Suddenly, almost breathless with a crushing pain, Cynthia's anger drained away, leaving her exhausted with frustration. She stepped into the elevator and jabbed frantically at the floor button, hot tears threatening to spill down her cheeks for the hundredth time that day. Only once the elevator door was safely shut did she let down her guard. *Damn it!* None of this was fair! It *wasn't fair* that James had lied to her, and it *wasn't fair* that Clara had betrayed her – she'd lost both her boyfriend *and* someone she had thought to be her friend in one morning. Overwhelming betrayal coupled with contempt for them both washed over her in a tidal wave of pain, the shock almost incomprehensible.

But most of all, she was angry with herself. She had allowed herself to be influenced, to be drawn into others' schemes and agendas, relied on their authority to help her instead of achieving recognition on her own merit. She knew her own capabilities, yet she had taken the easier, dishonest route.

Perhaps, she realised with a jolt, this was what she deserved. Her mother's voice came to mind, an echo from childhood: 'Cheats never prosper.'

She suddenly felt chilled with mortification. How could she ever explain this mess she had created to her parents? They loved her and had been so proud when she got the position at Clarence and Fulton. If she did go home, what could she possibly say? How would she face them? Cynthia sank to the floor of the elevator. She covered her face with her hands and her shoulders shook with sob after incandescent sob.

20

Changes

Kate cheerfully threw her belongings into her burgundy leather Anya Hindmarch workbag. It had been a special gift to herself, a rare celebratory treat for doing so well since arriving at the new office. She had just closed a lucrative deal, her third this month, and was quite enjoying working there. Her colleagues were great. None of the nastiness or one-up-man-ship she had experienced at the main office. Here it was all steady work, self-discipline and productivity, mixed with a daily dose of spirited banter among colleagues.

'OK! That's it for today!' her team leader's voice rang out. 'Well done, everybody! Especially Marc and Kate – another great week! See you all bright and early on Monday morning. Kate, could I see you for a moment before you go, please?'

Kate looked up expectantly. Her boss here was Carol McManus, an attractive, forty-something Scottish woman with strawberry blonde hair swept up into a neat high chignon, merry blue eyes and a wicked sense of humour.

On her first Monday, Carol had welcomed Kate in her

office and asked, 'What experience do you have? What salary do you expect?'

Her eyes had twinkled with jollity, so Kate realised she was being teased, but forced herself to straighten her spine and bravely request a higher rate than her previous contract.

'Well, what would you say to a package of six weeks' vacation, fourteen paid holidays, a company retirement fund to match fifty percent of your salary, private health care and a brand new company car leased every two years, say, a shiny red Audi?' Carol had responded.

Kate had blinked in surprise and, before she could check herself, blurted, 'Are you *kidding* me?'

Carol had retorted swiftly, without missing a beat, 'Yes... but you started it.'

From that moment, Kate had liked Carol and was pleased and proud to be working for her. She was someone you could be open and honest with, and as long as they worked hard, Carol supported her staff and was always ready to help where she could. Kate had been made to feel really welcome, with a salary increase into the bargain.

'I'll be right there, Carol,' she replied, wondering why she was being called into her boss's office.

'You'll be needing an apple if you're going to be teacher's pet!' Marc taunted with a cheeky grin.

Kate shot him a brief smile and disappeared into Carol's office.

* * *

Cynthia slowly packed up her belongings. It had been one hell of a month, but she had survived it. Learned a few things. Made one or two useful contacts, and even had a potential contract to chase up next week.

Stepping into the fresh air, the Friday feeling of freedom hit her and she smiled to herself. She had all weekend. No need to rush to the station today, it was a beautiful evening. Perhaps she'd wander to the sea. Have a coffee. Maybe treat herself to a new novel.

She made her way to the Barbican, Plymouth's waterfront area full of quirky little shops and buildings, to a new bookshop she had been planning to visit. She bought the new Renée Shafransky mystery and a takeaway cappuccino, and wandered along to the park, tired but calm and at peace. It was the first time in ages she had felt so settled and the fresh sea air and the hot, sweet coffee further relaxed her. Settling comfortably on a wooden bench, Cynthia placed her parcel and coffee next to her, stretched her arms and legs and arched her back. Warmed gently by the late day's sun, she allowed herself a small smile of satisfied reflection on recent events.

It had been such a tough time. She had learned some equally tough lessons.

Erik had generously given her two days off to think about what she would like to do, and told her she may contact him any time if she needed to. She had seen him in a different light, realised how compassionate and dedicated to his staff he was. She had the impression that although he was aware she had made serious mistakes and would not tolerate that behaviour again, she was entitled to another chance.

James had requested a transfer. He hadn't made any attempt to contact her, or even say goodbye. That hurt, but Clara had been right about one thing: he wasn't worth Cynthia's time or energy. Sitting in the warmth of the evening sun after working hard all week and making a little progress on being an accepted

– and even respected – part of the team, she allowed herself a grain of generosity towards him. She almost wished him well, but was glad she didn't have to see him again.

Kate was another matter. Cynthia winced at the memory of the damage she had caused. Her only explanation was jealousy and that was no excuse. She had sent Kate a simple text message: 'I'm sorry.' One day, she hoped, there'd be the chance to apologise in person.

Clara was Cynthia's biggest regret. She had trusted her, as a friend and a senior colleague. The last time they met, she had spat poison at her – and she was unlikely to see her again now she was transferring to Paris. Well, let her go. Maybe that was for the best. Clara had done enough damage. Cynthia had learned some valuable lessons from their former friendship, such as not using others, not taking without giving, and not being spiteful and self-obsessed. Erik repeatedly stressed that a great team was the most important asset a company possessed – everyone was valuable and everyone contributed to their success as a whole.

She was glad to have known Clara, grateful to her, even. From Clara, she had learned about the importance of hard work and commitment. Not relying on others to make it happen for her. She'd learned to respect herself, stand up for herself and recognise and work towards her own desires; achieve her own goals. Most importantly, she had learned not to use others but to work on developing her own judgment and intuitive skills to get the results she wanted.

And it was working.

Cynthia was really beginning to feel like part of the team, for the first time ever. It wouldn't happen overnight, she knew that. But she was completely, absolutely, one hundred per cent damn well sure she would make it happen! She wanted it more than anything.

Cynthia crossed her legs and took another sip of her coffee. Her future was brighter than ever, and she was grateful.

* * *

Driving home Kate usually turned the car stereo volume up high and sang aloud to her favourite tunes. Tonight though, she felt subdued and the music was low, background noise to her thoughts. She had plenty to think about. Carol was leaving her post to follow her husband's career, which would take them back home to the north of the country. She had suggested a few people she believed would fit the bill as potential leaders for the Crownhill office, Kate among them, but Kate didn't seriously expect to be considered. She had so much yet to learn and had only just joined the office. Besides, another change so soon would be quite unsettling and she wasn't sure she was ready for that.

It was wonderful to be considered, but Kate wasn't sure if she would apply for the position.

* * *

Lauren's phone burst into life just as she and Gretchen returned from their morning walk. The sky had darkened without warning and they were soaked from an unexpected heavy downpour. Thunder rumbled menacingly in the distance. A storm was brewing over the moors and Lauren was glad to have made it home before it broke.

She unclipped Gretchen's lead and threw a towel over her before she could shake water all over the hallway, then balanced on one foot while trying to take off her left boot.

Annoyingly, the zipper was stuck. She groaned in exasperation and hopped about, trying to forcibly wrench the boot off. At that moment her phone rang from the depths of her rucksack and she rummaged through the bag with her free hand while juggling Gretchen's lead, bag and wet towel while still wrestling with the stuck zipper.

'Good Morning, Lauren.' The deep, silken voice startled her into dropping the lead and overcoat on the floor. Her knees weakened and she sank helplessly to the bottom stair. Surely this couldn't be Greg Harrington phoning her? Lauren's heart skipped a beat. Maybe two. Possibly three.

'I hope I haven't called you too early?' He sounded concerned at the silence.

'G-good morning!' She almost laughed at the sound of her own shaking voice. 'Greg! Not at all! It's lovely to hear from you. What can I do for you?'

'It's rather what I may be able to do for *you,*' Greg joked. 'I may have found a suitable new place for Buddy, if his owners are still interested in re-homing him. Ben and Joyce Goodwin of Mill House Farm and their four children have been looking for a new companion, and Ben needs a strong dog capable of being outside all day in all weathers with him.'

'Oh, Greg, that's excellent news. It sounds just the sort of life Buddy would have chosen for himself, full of outdoor adventures and children to play with. I'm sure Craig and Julia will be so pleased. I'll call them and let them know.'

'Great,' said Greg. 'Saturday morning, then, if that suits you and your friends. I can swing by your place and pick you up and we can all introduce Buddy to his prospective new family.'

'I'll confirm that with you. Thanks so much.'

For ages after the call ended Lauren found herself smiling. Saturday. Something to look forward to.

* * *

Saturday promised to be mild, with a hint of spring in the air. Lauren woke early and at eight was by the window, waiting expectantly, Gretchen by her side. Her gaze wandered past her garden to the empty road and the sky above, now a timeless expanse of clear vibrant azure. A colour you could lose yourself in. The colour of forever.

At last Greg's Land Rover turned into the drive and Gretchen's ears twitched as she sat straight up, her tail thumping in happy anticipation.

'Yes! A visitor!' laughed Lauren and hurried to open the door. 'We're going with Greg to see Buddy's new home.'

Greg greeted Lauren warmly, then bent to say hello to Gretchen.

'Let's see how you're doing,' he said, and quickly examined her leg, running his hands firmly but gently over the foreleg that had been injured in the snow. 'All good,' he announced with a smile, and lifted her into the back seat.

As soon as Lauren was settled comfortably in the passenger seat, they set out to meet Julia, Craig and Buddy at Mill House Farm.

Driving through the narrow country lanes, curiosity created a deep aching void in Lauren. It was delightfully torturous to be so close to him. She wanted to know so much about Greg, and there were so many intimate and personal questions about his life she desperately wanted to ask - but knew she couldn't.

She strove to keep the conversation superficially light between them, but it took an effort and she was relieved when a large square farmhouse of red brick and grey slate tiles came into view. It had a slightly formidable look about it, standing alone on the side of the hillside, which was still flecked with drifts of white, like cotton candy against a backdrop of velvety green. Craig and Julia's car was already parked at the end of a roughly winding gravel path that snaked its way through the large vegetable garden to the back door.

Craig had Buddy on the lead, keeping a firm hold as the big mastiff strained to explore every rock and blade of grass in sight. Julia looked upset and uncertain, but Craig reached for her with his free hand and they all set off towards the house.

Greg rapped smartly on the painted wooden door. It was flung open and a cheerful barrage of laughter, warmth and golden light greeted them. A smiling woman in a bright pink T-shirt and faded ripped jeans ushered them inside.

'Come in! Come in! Don't mind the mess. Welcome!' She almost shouted over the top of the noise the children were making. 'Make yourselves comfortable if you can find a chair. Davey, eat your porridge nicely, there's a good lad – and *stop* teasing the cat! *Hannah!* Come help me clear the table!'

A large orange tabby cat with a crooked ear and a bombproof demeanour jumped down from the side of the table and flicked his tail in a devil-may-care manner, completely unconcerned at the presence of this large, strange newcomer in his kitchen.

The four excited children turned to look at the visitors, took one look at Buddy and, screaming with joy, hurtled towards him. Within seconds they had enveloped Buddy into their happy midst, fed him three biscuits and half a bowl of porridge and the cat had made it *quite* clear who was boss around here.

Lauren cast a concerned glance at Greg, unsure of the

chaos and clatter they had walked into, but he was standing back, straight and steady as any rock, with an amused, coolly confident smile.

Craig looked relieved and Julia's earlier concern had been replaced with a smile as she played with toys on the floor with Buddy and the two younger children.

After cups of tea and assurances that Buddy would be one of the family and Julia and Craig could visit any time as long as they were prepared to 'take us as you find us', they took their leave.

'Well, that seemed to go rather well!' Greg said, holding the door of the Land Rover open for Lauren. 'A good place for a big strong Rhodesian Ridgeback.' He took her hand and helped her up, his unexpected touch sending a thrill through her.

'Yes, I think Buddy has safely landed on all four paws there!' Lauren smiled. 'But I thought he was a mastiff?'

Either way, she felt a glow of satisfaction. Buddy would be safely cared for in a much more suitable home and Julia and Craig could relax and enjoy waiting for their new arrival knowing they'd made the right decision.

* * *

Driving back to Alverston Manor after dropping Lauren at home, Greg smiled contentedly. He was delighted to have been able to help the gorgeous Lauren and was truly appreciative he could chat so easily to her. He found himself mysteriously intrigued by her, she was such a contrast – so shy and reserved, yet with a natural kindness and warmth. Smart and sharp, too, capable of running her own business. He was sure she had hidden depths, like an iceberg. From the brief but pleasurable times he had spent with her, he had gained the distinct impression that what he had discovered so far was just the beginning, because it was almost impossible to read her thoughts.

One thing he did know, she was dating. He had seen her with that successful chap from the insurance world a few weeks ago at the opera, and their photo had been in the local paper. It was little wonder someone as special as her had a distinguished partner.

Thoughtfully, Greg flicked the car into cruise control. He had Josh to thank for Lauren drifting so unexpectedly into his life. Josh was often shy with new people but he'd really taken to Lauren. Greg smiled. And so had he. After the loss of his wife he'd become almost a recluse, choosing to dedicate his time and energy into building up his veterinary practice and being a devoted full-time father. Now he'd had time to heal and think perhaps there might be someone who would share his future. Even if Lauren was committed to someone else it had been such a pleasure today to converse so easily with such a special and intriguing woman.

21

Missing

Lauren was taking a welcome coffee break from making up the late afternoon deliveries, absent-mindedly watching raindrops make spattered patterns as they hit the shop window. A rainbow arched across the sky; the fading light played on the counter and reflected tiny prisms of colour from the crystal vases in the window display. Her phone's shrill ring broke into her peaceful daydreaming.

'Lauren?' Janelle's soft French lilt had an urgent tone.

'Janelle, what's wrong?'

'Look, it may be nothing… we are not sure. We think Josh and Rebecca may be missing. They went out walking all day yesterday, and were due back after their sunset picnic supper last night. When they didn't return, Greg and I thought they would be back this morning, but when he called in at the cottage this afternoon they still weren't there. We have tried to phone them, but there is no answer, most likely they are out of range or out of battery life. The phone signal can be so unreliable on the moors. Elaine and Paul haven't heard anything from them either.'

'Oh my goodness! You must be so worried! Janelle, have you told the police? Do you or Greg have numbers for Josh's friends? Maybe they left a message with one of them.'

'Greg has notified the police but we've heard nothing yet. They are seventeen and the police just think they are still out camping and will be home later. But it just doesn't sound like Josh to be so irresponsible. Something must have happened...' Panic added a tremor to Janelle's voice. 'I am so worried! Greg is talking about venturing out over the moors to try and find them.'

'That will be difficult unless you know precisely where to look.'

Lauren's practical side went into overdrive and her mind whirled with images as she recalled the location of so many childhood picnics and adventures. Her grandfather had taught her to be an expert at navigating some of the most beautiful moorland spots; but many were off the beaten track and full of treacherous marshland and this area was one of them.

'Janelle, where *exactly* did they go? Do you know?'

'Yes. Josh said they would go to the area where the ancient stones were discovered. Cut Hill. I don't know that area, but of course Josh and Greg know the moor so well. Do you know it?'

'Yes, I do.'

Inwardly, Lauren groaned. Cut Hill was a particularly high and desolate area of the moor surrounded by marshland. There were good walking tracks and some of the best views in the whole of Dartmoor, but no distinct roads or occupied buildings for miles. The couple might have got a lift part of the way, but they would have had to walk to reach the high viewpoint, which was the place they were most likely to head for. With the weather taking a turn for the worst and the light fading this was a perilous situation, fraught with danger at every turn. Trying desperately to keep the anguish from her voice, she explained the difficulties to Janelle.

'Hmmm… There are no real roads out there, and the terrain is heavy peat marshland. It's bound to be very wet and boggy after the storm last week. The old drover's track leading there can be difficult to find and follow safely. If Greg does try to drive out there, he might have to take quite an indirect route, because the storm last week will likely have made some of the track impassable.'

Lauren's mind spun and she found herself thinking aloud.

'Look, Janelle, try not to worry too much. The police could be right…they are probably just camping and enjoying themselves, and decided to stay out a little longer than expected and couldn't call because there was no signal. Ask Greg to wait until I have spoken to Elaine. She may have heard something by now. I'll get back to you as soon as I can.'

'Thank you, we appreciate your help. I'll be in touch if we hear anything.'

'Likewise. Speak soon.' There was a click from the other end as Janelle rang off.

Elaine sounded distraught. 'We haven't heard from her,' she said, 'and neither have any of her friends. We've called everyone we could think of, but no news.'

'OK, I know it won't be easy, but try not to worry. I'm sure we'll find them safe and well.'

Lauren hoped her voice sounded more confident than she felt. One thing she knew for certain; knowing Josh and Reba were out there somewhere, perhaps in trouble, she couldn't sit back and do nothing.

Leaving the shop in Julia's charge, she set off with Gretchen to Alverston Manor. On the way she spoke to Greg to tell him there was still no news from Reba.

'Nothing from Josh either.'

The quietly worried tone in his voice tugged at Lauren's heart. She could only imagine how he was feeling and didn't know how she could help, only that she would in any way she could.

The gates were open when she arrived so she made her way up the driveway and parked. The kitchen door was ajar and Lauren knocked, then tentatively pushed the door open. Janelle and Greg were sharing a brief hug.

'OK, dear, I'll be back later. If you need me just call,' Janelle said.

She swept past Lauren with a brief smile, her medical bag in one hand, heading for her car. Called out to clients, Lauren assumed. Business must go on. This must be incredibly difficult for Greg.

He turned to face her and Lauren's heart twisted. He looked so drawn and tired.

'Any news yet?' she asked.

'No. None of Josh's friends have heard from him since the morning they left, but the police want to wait another twenty-four hours before launching a search. I can't get through to Josh's phone, it goes straight to message bank. It's not like him to be unreliable. I am extremely worried for them both.'

Greg gripped the side of the table, his knuckles white and his mouth a straight line, worry and anxiety etched onto his face.

'There's been nothing from Reba, either. I am sorry. Greg,

what should we do?'

'I can't sit here and do nothing. Janelle was against it but I must go out and try to find them before it gets dark. I'll take the Land Rover.'

Lauren gasped. 'It's too dangerous to drive! Any attempt to find them would have to be from the air. You can't drive around the moors, especially at this time of year. It's far too marshy and there are only a few passable tracks. We could explore them of course. Josh would have taken one of them –'

'Lauren,' Greg interrupted, 'are you saying you know this part of the moor?'

'Like the back of my hand since childhood. But you *can't* drive there. Greg, please listen to me, you will be in danger and I couldn't bear it if something happened to you.'

She abruptly stopped and checked herself. 'I mean, if something were to happen to you, too,' she corrected, controlling the panic in her voice.

Thankfully, Greg was too worried and deep in thought to notice her blunder.

'There may be another way,' he said. 'Would you be willing to help me?'

'Of course. What had you in mind?'

Greg gazed out of the window. 'We have several hours of daylight left and while it is overcast, it's not raining. We could go on horseback, maybe… Lauren, do you think you could ride over the moor with me? Show me the route to Cut Hill you think they may have taken?'

Lauren paused, her body perfectly still but her mind in a whirlwind of turmoil. If she did this, full responsibility would be hers. If they were to survive – all of them – she couldn't afford to make a single mistake. She was a good rider, although it had been a few years since she'd been on a horse. Yet she was certain of her ability to ride steadily over the moors. She was also completely confident in her knowledge of the land; it would mean finding the safest route to steer them through the marshlands, still wet after the winter, and up to the higher ground where Josh and Reba were likely to have set up their evening camp.

'Yes, Greg, I believe I can,' she said quietly. 'I'm sure I can remember my way around that area of the moors very well. I think together we can do this.'

'Good. I'll sort out some riding gear and pack a few essentials. Make sure our phones are charged and let friends and family know what we're planning. We'll have to move quickly if we're to get there by evening. Lauren, you'll have to lead the way for me.' He studied her carefully. 'Are you sure about this? I need your help badly but don't want to pressure or bully you into this.'

He gently took her hand and Lauren felt an instant connection. Time and place faded into oblivion, only the here and now mattered. She looked directly into his eyes. There was no choice. The situation was desperate. Of course she was going to help this wonderful, special man whom she secretly loved to find his son who had once helped her. She nodded.

'OK, let's do this!' He grasped her arm in thanks, sending a thrill of anticipation through her, then called to old Tom the stable groom to saddle Aaron and Maya as quickly as possible.

* * *

Tom helped her mount the huge but patient and gentle Maya. Greg effortlessly swung into Aaron's saddle, the spirited stallion chewing at his bit and eager to be off.

Lauren hadn't ridden for years, but once in the saddle she found her confidence quickly returned. Besides, she had to do this; Josh and Reba needed them.

They set off together, Greg allowing her to set the pace but checking every few hundred yards to make sure she was OK. As she gained confidence, she allowed Maya to trot a little, then break into canter with ease, with Greg close on her heels.

To her relief, Lauren had no problem recalling safe passages through the marshlands and they rode in single file, Lauren leading the way. Despite the fact she knew the route and remembered it clearly, her heart thumped as Maya's great hooves splashed through the boggy mess. One slip and they would both be in trouble.

An ethereal haze arose from the ground around them, giving their world a strange, unearthly appearance. Ghostly cold finger-like tentacles of mist twisted around the horses' legs, as if trying to ensnare them. The two horses steadily plodded on, unfazed.

As they approached the Hill, the afternoon air took on a damp chill and the sky darkened to a deep purple. The air seemed to close in around them as they reached a fork in the path.

Lauren pulled her horse's reins into a dead stop, trying to ignore the anxiety and nausea swirling deep inside her. She sat statue-like in the saddle, as if paralysed with concentration, absorbed by her own thoughts and intuition; acutely aware she must now choose the correct route. There was no room for error.

She *had* to get this right.

Maya waited patiently, as if sensing she needed to stand still so Lauren could concentrate.

Greg drew up alongside her, his face drawn with anxiety. 'Which way?' he asked quietly.

Deep in thought, her mind whirling with the possibilities, Lauren didn't answer. Imagine…being seventeen, in the sunshine, enjoying life…which way would she go? Lost in concentration, she gazed unseeingly straight ahead, as if in a trance.

'Lauren, which way?' Greg's voice was patient, but there was an underlying urgency to his tone.

Lauren sat still and upright in her saddle, staring into the distance.

'OK. Let's see…' Greg frowned. 'I think Josh would have gone this way. The path is smoother and more even. It's easier by far. Lauren, let's go!'

'No.'

She slowly turned her head, speaking softly but firmly.

'What do you mean? What are you thinking? Tell me.'

'It's not that way, Greg. You're wrong. It's this way.' Her gaze fell towards the other path. 'I know that path is easier, but Josh wouldn't have chosen it. He wouldn't have gone for the easier route. In the sunshine, with a girlfriend he wanted to impress, he would have taken the higher more difficult path, so they could enjoy the view and the sunset together. And the physical climb wouldn't have been too difficult for them. He would have gone this way, I'm sure of it.

'OK,' he said quietly. 'Let's go up.'

Steadily and slowly now, the massive horses picked their way over the rocks, inching their way above the marshland and up the jagged, rocky path, the late spring evening air getting cooler and heavier. There was a light sprinkling of dew on the ground around them and evening was drawing in.

Lauren knew there was a ledge where campers often chose to stay; the sunrises and sunsets were stunning and they could see for miles around from there. But it was a few miles to go.

Suddenly, Maya stumbled and Lauren fell forward. She clutched the mare's mane in a desperate effort to stay on her back. Maya whinnied and danced, holding her left forefoot high. Greg dismounted and was at her side in a flash, ready to catch Lauren and soothing Maya with long, massaging strokes on her neck.

'I'm OK, Greg,' Lauren breathed, composing herself.

'I'll have to check her foot.'

'Here, let me help you.'

Lauren deftly swung her leg over Maya's broad back and launched herself blindly downwards, into the thick white mist and Greg's waiting arms. He caught her effortlessly, holding her a few seconds longer than necessary. Carefully he set her down and handed her Maya's reins.

Lauren's heart hammered in her chest, her emotions thrown into a swirling mixture of anxiety, worry and burning desire to comfort Greg. Holding the great horse steady and speaking to her quietly, she watched in awe as Greg lifted her massive foot to check for damage, and removed some broken rocks from her sole.

'She's sound,' he declared after a few moments. 'But I think it may be safer if we lead them on foot the rest of the way.'

Lauren breathed a sigh of relief. Another four hundred metres or so and they would be there. Painstakingly she counted the steps to herself.

One hundred... Two hundred... Three hundred... Surely they *had* to be getting close now.

'Hey! Help!' The call rang out above them, urgent and clear. 'Over here! *Help us!*'

'Josh!' Greg shouted. 'Josh, hold on – we're coming!'

Lauren moved to accompany him but he turned to her, shaking his head. 'Wait here with the horses. I can make it up there quicker by myself.'

Lauren watched his retreating back gradually disappear into the mist as Greg jogged the last few hundred metres of the path, his medical bag tightly grasped under his arm.

Alone in the quickly dimming twilight, Lauren was almost paralysed with an overwhelming sense of relief and exhaustion. Thank goodness they had made it here safely. Thank goodness they had found Josh and Reba. But it wasn't over yet. She shuddered in apprehension. They had to get back and it was growing dark.

After what seemed an eternity Greg reappeared from the shadows, cradling Reba in his arms. She was cold and exhausted, her right leg stiffly held out in front of her at an awkward angle. A makeshift splint was on her left leg and she was whimpering softly into Greg's chest with each movement. Josh followed looking mortified, carrying their backpacks.

'She slipped last night and hurt her ankle,' he said. 'I think it's broken. I tried to phone, but I couldn't get a signal. The batteries on our phones are flat now… I gave her soup and painkillers and strapped her ankle up as best I could. I thought it best to stay with her and keep her safe and wait for other people to come – but no one did…' His voice wavered and he sounded on the verge of tears.

'It's OK son, you did the best you could. You did the right thing,' Greg reassured him.

He lifted Reba up onto Aaron's broad back and then helped

Josh up behind her. Lauren and Greg set about tying the backpacks and solar lamps onto their saddles, the light from the lamps bathing their path in an eerie yellow glow. Greg handed Lauren and Josh a powerful torch each, which sent laser-like beams of white slicing easily through the darkness.

'Are you OK?' Greg looked at his son worriedly. 'We have to set off if we're going to be back down the hillside before dark.'

'Don't worry, Dad, I'll make it,' Josh set his jaw in brave determination.

Gingerly, the exhausted travellers wound carefully back down the hillside, Greg leading the gentle giant Aaron, who seemed to sense he had a precious cargo and adopted a calm, steady manner. Reba seemed comforted by the steady rhythmic sway of the horse's movements.

Maya followed her companion closely, nose to tail in the gloom. At times, Josh held Reba, supporting her weight to try and ease the pressure on her injured leg. Other times the exhausted young man walked, leaning against Aaron's great muscular flank for support.

The night air engulfed them, close and thick now; a tangible dampness clung to their clothes and hair, making it harder to move. The cold started to bite and work its way through their damp clothing into their bones and Lauren felt it chill her very soul. With skilful intuition, she led the great horses through the marshlands, plodding their way across the treacherous land and occasionally twitching their muscular flanks involuntarily, in an attempt to shake off the cold. She gave silent thanks for the bright lights that pierced the darkness and told herself that every step led them closer to safety.

And home.

22

Explanations

When they finally delivered their young charges to safety, it was very late and Lauren was too bone-tired to drive home. She thankfully accepted Greg's suggestion she take one of the rooms at the Manor. His housekeeper Dorothy immediately buzzed into action, preparing a guest room despite Lauren's protests that she did not wish to cause any trouble. Dorothy hushed her objections, fussing over details and dashing between rooms until she was satisfied she had thought of everything Lauren might need.

Lauren was so tired when she was eventually shown to her room that she simply stripped off her outer clothes and climbed gratefully into bed, where she fell into a deep, dreamless slumber.

Next morning as she slowly opened her eyes she quickly became aware she had slept far too late. Streams of pale lemon springtime sunlight streamed in from cracks in the heavy velvet curtains, illuminating tiny dust particles dancing in their sunbeam trails as if teasing her. She yawned and stretched blissfully. Then the previous night's events came rushing back to her.

Lauren sat up and took in her surroundings. She was in a gorgeous Queen Anne style room, with an expanse of embroidered cream brocade spread over a wide canopied bed. It was so comfortable, no wonder she had fallen into such a deep sleep immediately her head touched the pillow.

Someone had placed a bright posy of garden flowers next to an elegant tray laid with a china tea set on a dresser across the room. Lauren swung her legs over the side of the bed and felt the prick of goose bumps on her skin in the chill of the morning air. She padded over to the dresser, her joints stiff and aching from last night's riding, and poured a cup of steaming hot tea, thankful for the rejuvenating warmth and sweetness.

A small white hand-written card sat propped next to the flowers.

'Thank you for everything, love from Josh and Reba.'

She smiled at the thoughtful gesture. Josh must have picked the flowers from the garden earlier this morning. Judging by the light, it must be late morning. She had best shower as quickly as possible.

The quaint, elegant en suite bathroom filled her senses with comfort and a symphony of fresh lavender, citrus and rose emanated from the choice of soaps and candles. The chilly tiles underfoot gave way to a deep, fluffy mat, while a shelf full of neatly stacked, rolled-up towels sat next to a crystalline white and glass shower that gleamed invitingly to one side of the room.

Lauren tried the taps and powerful sprays of water immediately streamed from the shower. The scented air swirled thickly damp and steaming around her. Eagerly, she stripped off and jumped under the comforting jets, allowing the warmth to massage and ease her aching shoulders and back.

Lauren allowed herself a few precious minutes, absorbed in a cloud of blissful delight. It was so tempting to savour the constant pummelling of the water, which simultaneously soothed and invigorated, and she luxuriated in the silkiness of creamy lather sliding over her skin and down her back as she rinsed off.

Several minutes later, wrapped in luxuriously soft towels, Lauren finished blow drying her hair and quickly dressed in the jeans, soft cotton shirt and pretty pastel blue cashmere sweater she had found carefully laid out for her on an armchair.

She tentatively made her way downstairs, unsure of her surroundings and found herself in a wide lobby with a creamy marble floor. Silence engulfed her. There was no sign of anyone else about. She knocked on a solid oak panelled door but there was no answer.

She knocked again and when there was no response, twisted the brass doorknob and opened the door to what she discovered was a dimly lit library. The shutters were partially closed against the daylight and open books and writing materials were scattered across a large ornate oak desk.

Closing the door on the room, Lauren turned and walked across the lobby to try another door. This time as she opened the door she heard the muted hum of voices. She entered an empty dining room with a large polished walnut table at the centre. Matching chairs were scattered untidily, but there were no dishes lying around or any other evidence that it had recently been used.

Following the disembodied voices, Lauren found herself

facing another oak door, this one slightly ajar. Feeling bolder now, she called, 'Hello! Good Morning!' and pushed the door open. A small radio played in the corner of a kitchen, where dishes and tea things were scattered about the huge worn table and a saucepan sat on the large cherry red and brass Aga stove.

The delicious aroma of fresh baking tinged with cinnamon and fresh apples drifted towards her and she realised she was famished. She hadn't eaten since yesterday morning. Carefully, she cut a slice of freshly baked bread, still warm from the oven, and helped herself to a small china bowl of porridge from the stovetop.

As she ate, she admired the view from the kitchen window. The gorgeous garden scene framed by the window was as delightful as any painting. The open countryside beyond gave a sense of isolation, of being high above all others, cut off from reality. A butterfly alighted gracefully on the windowsill and rested there a few moments. Noticing the smallest details gave Lauren a sense of calming reassurance, made her realise this was only a small square of a great world; yet somehow it seemed to roll forever endlessly.

And there, unobtrusive yet as beautiful as any sculpture or work of art, was the mirage tree. Their special, enchanting tree, glowing silver in the morning sun. She took in the natural beauty, the irregularity of the lines of the branches, then gradually she widened her visual field to the surrounding bushes, shrubs and other trees.

Simply breathtaking.

She couldn't imagine anything nicer than waking up in this gorgeous old house and seeing the same beautiful countryside scene every morning.

She was certain she would never tire of it.

The sudden crunch of hooves on the gravel path drew her attention to the open kitchen doorway, where she caught a glimpse of Tom, the elderly groom walking Maya across the yard.

'Morning!' Lauren called cheerfully.

Tom stopped in his tracks and returned her greeting with a friendly smile and politely raised his hand. 'Morning, Miss. I'm just walking Maya here, Mister Greg asked me to check her left fetlock for soundness. Seems she's all good, aren't you, old girl?' He patted her gently on the nose and Maya bowed her great head towards him. Obviously great old friends, Lauren observed.

'I'm glad Maya is all right,' she said. 'We nearly took a tumble last night.'

'Yes, I know, Mister Greg told me all about it this morning. How are you after your adventures yesterday?'

'I am well, thank you, Tom. All suitably rested and recovered.'

'Aye, good to hear. Mister Greg was mighty pleased with ye, said you were mighty brave for a lass. He couldn't have found young Josh without you. Good job, Miss.' Toms' eyes twinkled in admiration.

'Oh, it was the least I could do. I'm just glad we found them when we did. Tom, do you know where everyone is? I haven't seen a soul so far this morning.'

'Aye, Mister Greg was called out at sun up to one of the farms and hasn't been back yet. Janelle is taking the pet clinic in town this morning. She left about an hour ago. Dorothy went to the market early and I believe young Master Josh is with his young lady in Tavistock hospital.'

Of course. Reba had been injured. The memory of Greg carrying her quickly came back to her. 'Thank you, Tom. I'll go to the hospital and see how she is.'

'Right you are, Miss.' Tom nodded respectfully and he and Maya moved steadily together towards the stables.

Lauren quickly rinsed her breakfast dishes, returned to the bedroom to fetch her handbag, then headed for the hospital.

* * *

Reba was propped up on a mountain of soft white pillows, a bright pink plaster cast on her leg and feeling much better. Josh was sitting by her bedside, holding her hand.

'Thanks a lot for what you did, Lauren,' he said.

'Yes.' Reba bit her lip. 'We were beginning to think that no one would find us.'

Lauren smiled at them both. 'Don't mention it. Here...' She handed a carrier bag to Reba. 'I bought you some things.'

'Oh, great! Thanks so much.' Reba exclaimed rifling through the bag, finding toiletries, magazines, puzzle books and pens and soft drinks. 'Ideal! That's so kind of you Lauren.' She smiled happily. 'I've been spoiled today.'

'So I see.' Lauren nodded approvingly towards the yellow roses and daisies and chocolates on her bedside locker. Josh shuffled his feet and looked down, his cheeks flaming.

'I can see you're in good hands here, so I'll get going.'

Josh stood up. 'Um...I will too. I promised to do some jobs for Dad.'

'In that case I'll give you a lift back to the Manor.'

He looked hesitant. 'It's out of your way.'

'Of course it isn't. Come on. And thank you for my gorgeous flowers. It was very thoughtful of you.'

Josh shrugged. 'That's OK. I picked them this morning. Dorothy put them in your room for me. Have you seen Dad this morning?'

'No. I think I missed everyone. Except for Tom. I saw him earlier. He said your dad was called out on a dawn visit and Janelle's running the small animal clinic today.'

'I think Dad wants to organise something. A thank you dinner or something a bit special for you. I heard him talking to Dorothy before he went out.'

'Ah! That's so kind of him, but it's really not necessary. I'm just relieved we got you both back safe and sound. That's reward enough for me.'

Lauren gave his arm a friendly squeeze. She was growing rather fond of this pleasant, considerate young man with his gentle manner. Thank goodness they had found him and Reba safe. The alternative did not bear thinking about.

When they arrived at the Manor, Josh suggested, 'Come in and stay for a while. I know Dad would like to see you. He talks so much about you.'

'Does he?' That was a surprise. And it would be a shame not to see Greg before she left the Manor, if only to thank him for his and Janelle's hospitality. 'I'll wait.'

Josh went to help Tom in the stables, saying he would be back later for tea, and Lauren put the kettle on to make a pot of tea. As she carefully lifted the boiling kettle from the Aga's hot plate, the Land Rover pulled up outside the kitchen. Greg was back! A thrill of excitement ran through her.

'Greg!' His name burst from her as he came through the door. She instinctively walked towards him, as if drawn by some invisible magnetic force. He dropped his medical bag at the door and smiled warmly, his arms wide in greeting for a brief hug of welcome.

It was wonderful to feel his arms tight around her, if only for a few precious seconds before decency commanded she peel herself away. Was it her imagination, or didn't he want to let her go? She dismissed the thought. Best not to read anything into it; it meant nothing. He was being kind to her as usual.

'I'm glad you are still here,' he said. 'I thought I might have missed you by now. I have to go back out again almost straight away but I wanted to come back, see you if you were here and check on Josh.'

His words sent a warm glow straight to Lauren's soul. She felt so at peace here at this beautiful old Manor House and everything had worked out well. Josh and Reba were safe and she felt blessed to have such wonderful friends. Being close to Greg completed a circle of pure joy for her.

'It's great to see you. I'm so glad I managed to catch you before I left. I wanted to thank you so much for your kind hospitality. The house is just beautiful, and it was very generous of you to have me stay.'

'Not at all. It was the very least I could do. Lauren, I really can't thank you enough for all you did last night.'

'Oh, I was glad to help. Really, it was nothing.'

'It meant *everything* to me,' Greg interrupted with quiet certainty. His voice was soft but the passion in his tone snapped her into instant awareness.

'I needed a miracle, and you came to me when I needed guidance and a true friend. *No one* else could have done what you did. When it mattered the most, you were just magnificent. I can't begin to imagine what would have happened if you hadn't had the courage to help me. Lauren, truly, I can't thank you enough.'

'You're welcome.' Lauren steadily held his gaze.

The sincerity of his words echoed through her mind, their intensity making her feel slightly dizzy. She loved him. The realisation grew in her like a rose opening its petals after the rain. Nothing could be more sure, more perfect or precise. She loved him completely. In all likelihood she would never love anyone else.

'Come have dinner with me,' he said. 'Tonight if you're free. Any evening you like. Please say you'll come.'

Lauren paused. His invitation reached out to her, coaxing and soothing. She wanted to so much, her heart literally *ached* to be with him – but it wouldn't be right.

'Greg, I'd love to. But I don't think I can. I'm sorry.'

His expression changed in an instant. He looked so sad Lauren thought her heart might break for him. But really, what else could she do?

'Hello, Dad!' Josh's cheerful voice rang through the kitchen, breaking the intensity of the moment. 'How was the farm visit?'

'All good. How are you feeling?' Greg turned his attention to his son.

They chatted for a few minutes and Lauren sipped her tea, then announced she had better be on her way. It was getting late and she had no excuse to prolong her visit, although she felt she could comfortably stay in this wonderful place forever.

'I'll walk you to your car, then I must get going,' Greg said.

'No, that's OK, really, I'm fine.' She smiled at him.

'I'll come with you.' Josh downed a glass of milk and banged the glass cheerfully on the sideboard. 'I've still got my coat on and I'm going back out to the stables anyway.'

Greg nodded in agreement. 'OK. And Lauren, once again, thank you so much. I should like it very much if you would reconsider about dinner and you are most welcome here any time.'

'Thank you.' She signalled Gretchen that it was time to leave. 'Perhaps we'll see you soon.'

'I hope so,' Greg said softly as he helped her slip into her heavy winter coat. 'Now I had best be going.'

As Josh and Lauren approached her car at the end of the driveway, Greg's Land Rover crunched on the gravel as it passed and he waved goodbye through the window.

Lauren shook her head. The past twenty-four hours felt surreal; could all this really have occurred since yesterday? So much had happened in such a short time. Last night she had set out with Greg on an extraordinary rescue mission. In contrast to the intensity of that experience, her morning here at the Manor had been peaceful and glorious. The memory of crossing the darkened moors on horseback in the freezing mist seemed to be fading into the distant past.

'Dad told me he wouldn't have found us without you,' said Josh when they reached her car. 'I'm so glad you were there or who knows what would have happened to Reba and me. I hope you will come by here again soon.'

'I will,' promised Lauren. 'I'd like to thank Janelle for having me stay as well.'

By then she might have her emotions under control. She did need to step back and take some time away from this glorious place and its missed opportunities. Oh, her heart ached to be leaving. If only things could be different...but there was no point dwelling on impossibilities.

'Great. Dad will be pleased if you come – even if you *are* dating that Erik guy. He'll be lonely again once Janelle goes back to France next month. You could bring Gretchen again, she loves it here.'

Lauren froze, mid-step. 'Josh, what did you say?' Had she heard him correctly? 'Janelle's going back to France?'

'Yes. It's a pity. I like her. She's been a great partner here but she wants to go back to her folks in France, so Dad will need another senior assistant. I think he'll miss the company, and he'll certainly miss the help. Since Mum died he's been on his own. That's why I want to qualify, so I can help Dad run the practice.'

'Assistant?' Lauren frowned. 'So… Janelle is your father's *business* partner? She's employed to live and work here?'

'Yep. She was telling me about her family and some boyfriend back in Bordeaux. It sounds great over there. When Reba's better, I'm going to ask Dad if we can go visit her sometime.'

Lauren leaned against the car. With overwhelming clarity, she realised she had got it wrong, jumped to her own conclusions. The special birthday bouquet; seeing them together at the theatre and at the Valentine's Ball. All this time she had believed Janelle and Greg were a couple, romantic partners for life, but they were business partners, friends, and companions – nothing more. Her mind whirled with the implications. Lauren turned and looked longingly at the house.

'Are you OK?' asked Josh.

'Ye-es,' she finally managed, fighting down a dreadful feeling of despair. She had got it completely wrong… she'd let Greg slip through her fingers…

Unthinkable! She felt numb with the realisation. She had turned down a dinner invitation from the one man she truly loved. Worse still, it sounded like he believed she was still dating Erik. Should she return to the house and wait for him? What would she say? Eventually, she turned her gaze to Josh.

'Josh, I'm not dating anyone. Not now.' She took a deep breath. 'Would you please tell your father I'll phone him later? Tell him… I'd like to reconsider his offer of dinner, if I may.'

23

Returned

Erik looked at his watch for the fifteenth time in eight minutes. Didn't that mob at the Crownhill office realise he was on a tight schedule here? They had an end of financial year deadline to meet, and they had promised to send the head of their Sales and Contracts team with their statistics for the past six months promptly by eleven a.m. *sharp.*

Dammit. It was two minutes past eleven now, and still no sign of him. The morning had been fraught with difficulties already.

Who was this guy anyway? Erik paced the office like a caged predator, all tension and taut nerves. He knew there had been some staff restructuring there recently, but it had happened while he was in London working on some major deals, so he hadn't been involved. Whoever it was, they had a bloody nerve, keeping him waiting like this.

Annoyed, he stood with his back to the door, looking out of the window for distraction. He took a deep breath. And another. *Why* was he so stressed? The London contracts had gone well. The changes he'd initiated had all been carried out. His team was working well. Their yearly statistics were *amazing*, had superseded the board's expectations. Erik knew he had everything under control.

It was time for a break, he realised. Little annoyances were getting to him. He had worked hard for a long time and had promised himself a trip home as a reward. He needed to welcome his new second-in-command and get him up to speed, then he could take off on sabbatical for a few months. The new guy arrived next week, Lucas Deverell. Some hotshot who had been headhunted by Clarence and Fulton's senior management from a rival company in London. Erik had heard of him. A family man with a pleasant, steady demeanour and a great reputation; apparently he'd jumped at the chance of a promotion with Erik's team and relocate his family to the beautiful southwest countryside.

Erik's door clicked open quietly and closed again. Didn't anyone knock these days? Spinning on the spot, his jaw clenched, he felt ready to tear strips off whoever it was.

Then he froze. Literally froze.

The air around him felt suddenly charged with electricity, as if a lightning bolt had directly struck his desk. Any tension was instantly dispelled.

Before him stood the most gorgeous red-haired girl with smiling emerald eyes and flawless Celtic skin. Standing tall in three-inch heels, her tiny waist accentuated by the perfect cut of her designer suit, she daintily glanced at her watch to give him a moment to recover.

'Good morning, Erik. It's nice to see you again. Maria told me you were keen to start so I showed myself in. Let's begin, shall we?'

Kate confidently flourished her statistics files and dropped them lightly on his desk. 'Mind if I take a seat?'

'Please do,' he said and with some reluctance turned his attention from the captivating woman in front of him to the files on his desk.

All the while he studied them he was acutely aware of her. There was a different air about her now. Clearly, young Katie had grown in confidence and self-assurance and she had obviously worked hard.

The Crownhill office had improved dramatically. In a few short months Kate had turned the productiveness of the sales and contracts teams around and their figures were incredible. As was hers, he couldn't help thinking before getting his mind back on track.

He had to hand it to Kate. He had hoped she would inject some new life into their second office and bring up their standards but he hadn't expected such phenomenal results in such short time. The board would no doubt recommend her for a well-deserved promotion any day now.

'At this rate, your team's results will soon supersede mine.' Leaning back in his leather swivel chair, he clasped his hands behind his head and stretched his legs under his desk. 'That will not do. I cannot allow your branch office to become more productive than my office.'

'Oh?' A small frown creased her forehead.

'You must understand,' he continued sternly, 'I will not let you overshadow me and my team. It will not happen. Not at any price. No way. Not in this lifetime.'

She leaned forward, ready to rise to this challenge and fight to defend her team and their achievements. 'But, as you can clearly see -'

'No!' He interrupted. '*Never.* Unless… you agree to have dinner with me tonight.'

She relaxed back in her chair and regarded him with a bemused smile. 'Fortunately, I am free this evening.'

'Excellent. Eight o'clock at Reubens. I'll ask Maria to book their best table. Exceptional effort deserves a reward.'

* * *

Here she was again. Back at the beautiful old manor she loved. Lauren stepped out of her car and took a few precious minutes to wander the garden, now bathed in a weak golden light from the sunset, which gave it a strange unworldly appearance. There was no sound except for a few songbirds in the boughs of the trees high above her, performing their last arias before settling for the night. Heady scents of jasmine and rose enfolded her in their embrace and she inhaled deeply, feeling her body and soul fill with a rare tranquillity and peace.

She always felt so relaxed here. Accepted. As if she truly *belonged,* somehow. Happily, she made her way to the kitchen entrance. She was confident here now, she knew her way around the Manor quite well. As she rounded the corner, Greg walked hurriedly to meet her.

'Welcome back!' he smiled, speaking in his usual quiet, reserved manner but his eyes betrayed his joy. 'I am so pleased you decided to come.'

'I'm pleased to be here!' She returned his warmth with a joyful smile of her own.

They walked towards the house and when Greg pushed open the door, Lauren felt a familiar welcome enfold her as she stepped into warmth radiating from the Aga oven and the scent of baking filled the air. She followed him through the kitchen to the hallway and he held the dining room door open for her. The long table was tastefully set for two and a posy of blossoms freshly picked from the garden adorned the centre.

'Greg, it's lovely!' Lauren exclaimed. 'I hope you haven't gone to too much trouble.'

'It's no trouble at all.' He took her coat. 'I enjoy cooking and spending time at home, I just don't often have the chance. Please – just make yourself comfortable.'

She settled into a chair and accepted a glass of wine. Greg joined her while their dinner finished cooking. He studied her thoughtfully from across the table.

'All this time, I thought you were dating Erik Danielsen. I saw your picture in the local paper. It was no surprise. After all, I figured there was no way in the world that someone as beautiful and special could possibly be alone. I had no reason to suspect you were no longer together.'

Lauren felt the heat rise in her cheeks and her pulse quickened. 'Thank you. But that relationship ended quite quickly. It was obvious we weren't suited. I love my home in the countryside and, well, his whole life is centred on socialising and travelling from city to city. I wanted so much to come to dinner when you first asked me, but I was still dating Erik then and when you ordered forty-eight red roses for Valentine's Day, I thought...'

'They were our business's contribution to the charity fundraiser. My practice always supports the Lions Club every year in any way we can and this year they requested help with the decorations. It seemed fitting to fill the order for the two pedestal decorations at the main entrance from a local business. I like to give back to the local community where possible, so we chose your shop. I think it's important to support any local community events, especially charity fundraisers. Janelle wanted to go to the opera and the Valentine dance, although of course, she has no one here to go with; so I escorted her. It didn't seem right she should go alone; besides, she didn't know her way around Plymouth very well at the time. She's been a great asset to us and I'm very glad she came to work here, but her time with us is coming to a close. And while she will be missed, it was always a temporary working arrangement. I will have to find a replacement, and quickly!'

So that's why he had chosen pink roses for Janelle's birthday, not red. They were a birthday gift and thank you for a friend and respected colleague, not a romantic partner. Her mother's words came to mind: 'You should never make assumptions; you don't know what life might have in store for you.'

'Lauren!' Greg's eyes twinkled mischievously. 'Surely you didn't think I would ask you to dinner here if Janelle and I were together?'

'Well, I know that *now,*' she laughed. 'And while I might have got *that* wrong, at least I know a ridgeback from a mastiff…'

She let the comment hang in the air until he realised what she had said.

He stared at her uncertainly at first then a hesitant smile played across his handsome features. He looked younger, Lauren noticed, almost youthful. The resemblance to Josh was striking.

'I see!' he bantered. 'Well, I guess you won't be wanting any dinner then. I mean, how could you possibly accept hospitality from someone so inept? Ah! I should have guessed. Oh, well, if that's the way it will be…'

She laughed and reached for his hand across the table and he clasped her hand with his own. Their eyes met, and for a few seconds they stayed quietly locked together in the happiness of their own private world.

'Come with me,' he spoke softly. 'Dinner isn't quite ready yet and I'd like to share something with you.'

Lauren nodded. She would've followed him anywhere.

Taking her by the hand, Greg led the way around the side of the great house and through the garden, which was now an abundance of colour and lush greenery; through the cottage garden of rose and camellia blooms, to an open, naturalistic realm where formal symmetry gave way to borders full of warmly scented herbs and wildflowers.

Suddenly, before them was their old silver birch tree, beautiful and serene, now budding with the promise of new life. Its silver paper-thin bark glowed faintly against the backdrop of emerald hills and clear azure sky; its shadow seemed to reach out and encircle them, with all the fond endearment of an old friend, in the glow of the softly golden evening sunshine. Lost in thought, Lauren reached out to touch the bark fondly, then leaned her full weight against the trunk, drawing the comfort of inner peace from its strength.

'OK, penny for them.' Greg smiled and handed her a wild rose as he walked over to her side. 'What are you thinking?'

Lauren took the rose. 'Thank you. Well, just how wonderfully familiar this place feels to me now.' Everything might be changing, but standing here, she knew some things would stay the same forever.

'I'm glad. I'd like you to feel at home here. I'd like you to come and see us much more often.' His voice was low and he leaned closer. She could hear him breathing and caught the heartfelt meaning of his words.

'I have a feeling I will.'

Her own breath was shallow, like whispers, and she turned to him. 'After all, some things are *meant* to be…'

His eyes on hers, Greg placed his arm around her waist and gently pulled her over to him. She willingly let herself be guided to him, the rose falling from her fingertips as she felt his hand on the side of her face, his thumb gently caressing just below her ear. She ran her fingers lightly down his spine, pulling him closer until there was no space left between them and she could feel the reassuringly steady beat of his heart against her breast.

His lips met hers, gentle and tentative at first, more comforting and soothing than words could ever be, then fervently, with increased yearning with every passing second. The birdsong, heady scent of jasmine and golden warmth from the evening sun all faded away until she was completely unaware of her surroundings. Everything had disappeared except the two of them, their bodies, hearts and souls entwined at the beginning of a journey that was as unique as it was perfect.

24

Blessings

'So, Elaine had a little girl? That's a wonderful blessing indeed!' Shirley smiled at the news as she buzzed around her kitchen, preparing salad and slicing freshly baked bread. Lauren poured chilled Pinot Grigio into glasses, enjoying the way the sun from Sherian's large kitchen window played on the crystal, making tiny prisms of colour that danced and flickered with the movement of the wine. 'So now they have their little boy and a new baby daughter – one of each.'

'Yes, and she's beautiful, Mum. Elaine promised to stop by this evening so you'll have a chance to meet her. Julia's baby is due in a couple of months too. They have signed up for mother and baby classes together.'

Could anything be more perfect?

'Reba is going to help in the shop while Julia is away, and Josh says he'll help with the deliveries if needed, until they start college.'

'It's all worked out beautifully then.' Shirley took a sip of her wine and turned to the oven. Slipping on her oven gloves she produced pies, baked potatoes, a quiche and batch of golden pastries.

'Hi there! We're here!' Kate's voice, ever cheerful, resonated from the hallway.

'Well, obviously,' Lauren retorted and rolled her eyes in mock annoyance.

She gave her sister a hug then pulled away and stared at her in admiration. She certainly had blossomed into a beauty. She looked fantastic, her shining red hair offset by a new navy blue faux fur-trimmed Lilly e Violetta coat. As Kate handed their mother a posy of flowers and a bottle of champagne, her pink diamond engagement ring sparkled in the light. Behind her, looking slightly sheepish behind a huge pink teddy with a candy-striped bow around its neck, Erik stood in the dimly lit hallway.

'Come!' Kate merrily signalled to him to follow her, and handed him a glass of wine.

'Yes, come on in, Erik, we don't stand on ceremony here.' Shirley extended her arms in welcome to her future son-in-law. 'Make yourself at home.'

'Kate, you look *amazing!*' Lauren said. 'But you must be roasting inside that coat.'

Kate giggled. 'I know. It's a bit warm for this time of year, but I couldn't help wearing it. I want to show it off. It's for our trip to Norway. I can't believe we leave tomorrow. I'm so excited to meet Erik's family.'

'Well, it looks just lovely on you. Here, Erik, give me that bear and make yourself comfortable. Kate, we ought to put that champagne on ice. Lauren, give me a hand to set the table, please.'

The kitchen burst into cheerful activity and laughter and

chatter filled the room. The giant bear sat drunkenly propped up in a rocking chair in the corner of the room, waiting for Elaine to claim him for her baby.

Muffled voices at the door and a sharp rap heralded the arrival of Elaine, Craig and their family. Josh and Reba had arrived too. Lauren flung the door open and ushered her friends in to the party.

As Elaine lifted the baby from her stroller, Kate and Lauren cooed in unison over her.

'Isn't she the most precious thing ever?'

'So adorable!'

'Perfect little fingers and toes.'

'Elaine, she's just *beautiful!*'

Shirley pressed a couple of coins into the baby's palm, for 'good luck, wealth and prosperity'. Elaine was delighted with the bear and Lauren produced a shiny red toy truck for Matthew to play with, which he promptly pushed all over the stone kitchen floor. Erik and Paul took their wine and retreated to the side of the kitchen, observing the cheerful chaos around them.

'Lauren, where's Greg?' Elaine asked.

'He's on a call to a client. He'll be here as soon as he can.' Lauren smiled. She had been looking forward to this evening ever since her mother had suggested a special dinner and family get together before Kate and Erik left for Norway.

They all settled at the table, talking excitedly about Kate and Erik's planned travels and Elaine and Paul's new family routine over hot soup and fresh bread. Lauren heard a knock at the door despite the chatter and hurriedly left the group. A few moments later, she returned, leading a slightly reticent Greg by the hand.

'Hello Greg! Welcome! So glad you could make it!'

Various greetings rang out from across the table and were met with a polite nod from Greg and happy smiles from Lauren. Shirley stood and briefly hugged him, then took his coat and bade him make himself comfortable and help himself.

After the meal, Paul, Greg and Erik shared a joke and an after dinner drink while Kate and Lauren helped their mother clear the table. The group settled down to a pleasant evening of coffee and playing cards. Josh and Reba took little Chester and Grace for an evening walk and Elaine retired to the parlour to feed the baby. As the evening turned into night, the party slowly broke up. Kate and Erik announced they had an early start the next day and ought to leave. Kate still had to finish packing before their travels. As they reached the door, Lauren hugged her sister fondly.

'Take care of yourself, Katie. Please phone and don't forget – we will be *dying* to know all about Norway and we expect dozens and dozens of photos.'

Lauren had tears in her eyes. Could this really be her little sister? She was all grown up and taking charge of her life.

'Aw, Laurie. I wish you could come with me. I'll miss you *every single* day. Of course I'll write. Distance won't ever pull us apart. I'll probably send you a hundred messages from the airport.'

After everyone else had left Lauren offered to help her mother with the last of the clearing up, but Shirley waved her away. 'No, it can all wait until tomorrow. It's late. I'll see you in the morning.'

* * *

Standing together in the peace of the garden, surrounded

by the tranquil stillness of the cool night air, Greg slipped his arm around Lauren's shoulders. She leaned against him, her head on his shoulder, and looked up at the expanse of black velvet, drinking in the beauty of the heavenly diamonds. Her face was softly lit by the silvery moonlight and Gretchen sat patiently at her side.

'I love the night-time. It's as if the whole world has turned into a mysterious and fascinating place.'

'Well, that's a good thing,' Greg said. 'A very good thing, as it happens. Because if you marry a vet, you will have to get used to late nights and early mornings.'

She smiled in absent-minded contentment and took a step towards her car. Suddenly the words he had spoken registered and she turned back to him in delighted surprise.

Greg stood perfectly still, looking up to the heavens, his hands firmly in his coat pockets. He carefully traced the smooth outline of the little leather-clad box in his left pocket. It had taken him the best part of the afternoon to choose it, but in the end he knew the simplest design was the right choice. A perfect brilliant cut solitaire with diamond encrusted shoulders. He had waited for this moment for a long time; not so long ago he had resigned to himself to defeat, believing it was impossible. His heart beat in anticipation and his mind filled with nervous excitement.

He had known from the first moment of meeting her that she was to be his future – if she would allow it.

At his words, Lauren's heart skipped a beat. She studied his face, her own lips curving upwards at the reserved smile playing at the corners of his mouth. 'I take it that's a proposal?'

'It is.'

The thrill of quiet excitement rose within her as she

allowed herself a glorious moment to think of the future and the promise of many wonderful, as yet unspoken, possibilities to come. Despite the inky darkness it was as if the whole world had started to shine and the dismal grey clouds of the past were fading, chased away by the brightness of destiny's promise of hope, for all their dreams yet to be fulfilled.

Karin Elizabeth Rose Smale

Typically Aquarian, Karin is an advocate of life on her own terms. She loves singing, dancing (she has been known to make the odd appearance on stage as a solo burlesque artist) is a student of the viola (when her neighbours are at work) and has a lifelong fascination with astrology – does this make her a majestic musical mystic? Twenty-something years as a Registered Nurse has made her a Master of Life and Understanding People. With Honours. She is staunchly humanitarian, vegetarian, libertarian and possibly a few other 'arians' as well.

She would like to take this opportunity to thank her readers and hopes you enjoy her work!

www.ingramcontent.com/pod-product-compliance
Lightning Source LLC
Chambersburg PA
CBHW021425110726

47901CB00008B/2296